The Key Party

The Key Party

James Gilbert

Creators Publishing
Hermosa Beach, CA

THE KEY PARTY
Copyright © 2017 James Gilbert

Cover art by Peter Kaminski

CREATORS PUBLISHING
737 3rd St
Hermosa Beach, CA 90254
310-337-7003

Library of Congress Control Number: 2017935934
ISBN (print): 978-1-945630-50-7
ISBN (ebook): 978-1-945630-48-4

First Edition
Printed in the United States of America
10 9 8 7 6 5 4 3 2 1

Contents

Acknowledgments

The act of writing is always a solitary undertaking — or, at best, a dialogue between the author and his imagination — but the creation of a book encompasses a community of friends and critics. Without them — their encouragement, support and sharp eyes — this work would never have appeared. I want to thank in particular Jonathan Auerbach, Jackson Breyer, Saverio Giovacchini, Ingalisa Schrobsdorff, Jim Cassell, Sari Hornstein and John Greven. Working with David Yontz at Creators Publishing was a great pleasure, and I am grateful for the improvements he made. I am also indebted to the many other friends and acquaintances who listened patiently as I explained why an author of several works of history who has spent years teaching about American culture would feel the wish and the need to turn to fiction writing. I hope that the result justifies my reasons.

~~~

Chapter 1

The first house on Golf View Court stood like a lonely sentinel on a rise of green surveying a larger flat square of waist-high brown prairie grass. Across the street, another house rose up, and behind it, barely visible through a curtain of tall trees, lay another patch of shimmering emerald, the mounded green of the fifth hole of the Protestant golf course. This (informal) religious designation of Fair Green Country Club and its membership limits was unusual even for this decade of tribal exclusions. But it was one of the unspoken rules of town etiquette that Catholics and Jews, though they were tolerated in small numbers as residents and could hold minor offices (the police chief was Irish, for example), could never be members, not of the club or really of the community as such. There was logic to this order of things, for it kept relationships distant and cordial. With everyone knowing one's place in such a small town, transgressing the rules on occasion with an act of kindness revealed a generosity of heart and spirit that would be much-remarked-upon and remembered. A pleasant word, neighborliness or, once every so often, an invitation to an informal dinner or cocktail party brought nods of approval from the leaders of society, who understood that such condescending democracy only strengthened the divisions that maintained a pleasant atmosphere of joint endeavor, as well as steady property values.

This ordering of sorts may have seemed extraordinary and severe, and perhaps the younger generation, which was learning about the new United Nations in the early 1950s and singing songs of world brotherhood in public school, may have wondered about the restrictions and covenants of Potawatomi Acres. (The town was named after local Indian tribes dispersed from their land by warfare and the federal government.) But this was probably a generational perception, because parents, teachers and figures of authority with a stake in the town (it was, after all, their property invested, not just with money but with moral conviction) believed fervently in the good life of the suburbs. Where else could one possess a patch of real estate, a small manse in a community of the like-minded and similarly accomplished? Having migrated from small towns, with their tangled skein of family feuds and age-old rivalries and disputes and their relentless monotony, these suburbanites had first fled to the city. But finding that place even more troublesome than the rural corners they had abandoned, they simply kept moving outward, putting down no roots or permanent ties until they reached this edge of the world, where they built a new place out of the brick of ambition and mortar of nostalgia. Thus, the town center looked as if it belonged someplace else, perhaps in an English village — or rather, it was more the idea of an English village, with a town square, a rail station for commuting husbands to Chicago and a row of small stores jostled against one another, offering the basics of food, clothing and services. Over these stores, under the sloping eaves and behind the half-timbered walls in the second story were the dental and doctors' offices, real estate and accounting businesses. Although there was a certain call for psychiatry — that distressing new branch of medicine — even if it was the subject of rumor and cocktail party jokes, no office had yet to migrate out to meet its needy clientele. For such appointments, there were noonday trips to Chicago, under the guise of shopping at Marshall Field's or having tea after a matinee symphony. It was not that analysis was shameful; indeed, for those who could afford weekly sessions, it had become almost a bragging right or a medical excuse to talk about oneself. But somehow, to locate the practice in Potawatomi Acres would have been tantamount to admitting that perhaps there was something in the town conducive to neurosis and melancholy. And that admission might open a flaw in the very fragile vessel of suburban life. And from there, where could one migrate to put the broken pieces of community life together again?

The only institution to rival Fair Green Country Club for its inclusiveness and prestige was the Potawatomi Community Church, a religious body that made few creedal demands on its members — aside from a vague hostility to Romanism — and belonged to no discernable denomination. Its principal tenets were belief in belief itself and faith that good would come to those who upheld community standards. If its membership overlapped almost entirely with that of the country club, the height of its activities was the seasonal opposite, centering around Christmas, Easter and, most importantly, "Donor's Sunday," which generally fell around Easter and the end of Lent as the harsh winter that prohibited golf softened. On this annual occasion, the Reverend Richard White discovered the pressing need for a new stained-glass window, repairs to the roof or new furnishings for Fellowship Hall, where he led the town's Boy Scout and Girl Scout troops on Fridays and Saturdays. Inevitably, there were a few intensely devout members who sorely tested Reverend White's knowledge and tolerance for Scripture and doctrine, but in the main, he performed as a master of ceremonies for baptisms, the welcoming and initiations of new members, weddings, funerals, and Scout initiations. He depended upon a volunteer organist and choir mistress, a graduate of Juilliard in New York who found herself, with nothing to do, in Potawatomi Acres, having followed her husband there. Miss Pinkham — she insisted on her celibate name as a title — led an adult choir consisting largely of sopranos and altos, with a smattering of unconvincing tenors, as well as a children's group that sang at Christmas, Easter and Donor's Sunday services. Together the church and the club rounded out the year and encompassed the moral and recreational circumference of the community.

There was also a public school, attended by most of the sons and daughters of Potawatomi, although a few additional children were bused in from outlying farms, smelling of fresh air, animals and the sweat of chores. A tiny Catholic school, attached to St. Jerome's Church at the edge of town, accommodated the offspring of that faith. Unlike the case with the more exclusive and older northern suburbs, no families sent their children to private academies. There was no need. And if there were any politics in town, they consisted mainly of complaints about corruption in Chicago and intense dislike of the Democratic governor, Adlai Stevenson, for the village was incorporated in city manager–style government, which ensured the practice of good business. Every other belief had the character of informality and private adherence, for Potawatomi residents demanded only adherence to the general principles of conformity.

However, for the town's most avid and insightful observers — its generation of high-school students — the subject of "life in the suburbs" was sure to generate an enthusiastic and ironic discussion. Having known nothing else, and with only the experience of day trips to Chicago museums or maybe one of the ballparks, they imagined that these discussions resembled the daily conversation of prisoners longing for the life on the "outside." Perhaps it was for this reason that petty crime was so immensely attractive — either the imagination or the doing of it. As a matter of course, Halloween nights were an invitation to reckless behavior — broken windows, upset trash cans, trampled gardens and the occasional brick thrown at a parked police car. But this was trivial in comparison with what could be imagined. The most common lawbreaking was underage drinking, in a state that equated adulthood with the age of 21. Consequently, there was almost a Saturday night parade of gleaming hardtop convertibles packed with teenagers driving to the slum in the next town over to find an itinerant drunk to buy illegal liquor. Indeed, this became so regular an occurrence that there was always a group of ill-kempt men lurking around the door of a seamy package-liquor store, waiting for a half-dollar tip for the purchase of a six-pack of beer. Everyone in the town knew, of course, but no one seemed to care because there were so many other rules to break, such as curfews and the additional regulations imposed by parents and schools and churches. Indeed, there were so many guidelines for youths that it was almost impossible to avoid stepping over someone's black marker.

Such minor incidents of juvenile crime, however, satisfied no one among this young cohort, and whenever the teens met in someone's rec room, the subject of suburban life and escape from it invariably came up. The word "conformity" was bandied back and forth in these talks like badminton birdies. In fact, it was so often a subject of conversation among boys (second only to girls and sports) that there was the danger that without constant complaining, this group of young people would quickly exhaust speech altogether. How could adults — their fathers and mothers — possibly be content in such a place, this terminus of their flight into boredom? Not, of course, that anyone cared much about adults or inquired seriously into the nature of that species except in the singular case when divorce was rumored. Indeed, mothers and fathers often seemed to be not adults at all but rather like older and indulgent friends with whom one happened to live. If they argued, drank too much, cried bitter tears or sat in stony silence around the dinner table, well, these were simply, it seemed, the habits of the type. To imagine them as passionate lovers was impossible and never mentioned. After all, how could they "do it" in bedrooms with twin bed sets separated by 6 feet of cold space, about the length of a coffin?

There were town rumors, certainly, that even reached the innocent ears of teenagers, particularly about one female golfer, a tall blonde, Mrs. Smith, with a loud liquid laugh and habitual white or baby blue Angora sweaters stretched tight against her sharp, up-pointed breasts. She was a perennial distraction from the somber game of golf, whose male devotees lived for bright and warm summer weekends. (Serious attendance at the local Protestant church only began after Thanksgiving and ended with Easter.) Mrs. Smith drew men to her table on the veranda overlooking the 18th hole, where she positioned herself on weekend afternoons, stretching out her fine bronzed legs. Often, the boys who caddied as a summer job lingered after being paid off for an extended look at this spectacle. Around her there was frequently the sound of cleats scraping on the flagstones in gentle harmony with the clink of ice as she swished her Tom Collins. She was a welcome sight to the tired golfers as they trudged off the course, silently cursing the duffs, shanks, lost balls and missed putts. Her friendly gestures were an invitation to forget this tribulation and imagine the delights of a brief and harmless flirtation. Frequently, one of the bolder men sat with her and recounted the misfortunes of his game. Certainly, she knew golf banter well, and she played every Wednesday afternoon — Ladies' Day — and was rumored to have a small handicap. But no male golfer, whatever the invitation or temptation, would ever agree to play on Ladies' Day. Two reasons were always given: Women played too slowly, and the tees were set forward to unfairly shorten the holes. But there was another compelling and unstated reason: A woman with a meticulous short game and accurate putts might actually outscore a companion driven to wild and careless shots by her tedious and studied play. The rumors swirling about Mrs. Smith, however, had nothing to do with the game or handicaps or Ladies' Day; they were about the possibility that this blond, divorced temptress might hook and slice a married man.

The most regular of foursomes who played on Saturday or Sunday mornings was a quartet of friends who lived along the stem of Golf View Court, which ran from the edge of the fifth green to the seventh tee, where the street dead-ended. They were as steady associates as could be found in the community — or perhaps any other

— and among its most respected citizens. There was nothing obvious other than proximity to explain their closeness, for they were very different in circumstance and occupation. Dan Clements, a downtown Chicago lawyer, Jim Reilly of Reilly Realty, Steve Watson, the manager of the local bank, and Teddy Barr, the aging ex-golf pro and insurance salesman, were as fast friends as their wives — the quartet of "golf widows" who regulated their husbands' social lives through elaborate and extended telephone calls and morning kaffeeklatsches when the children were at school or at summer camp. There was one other couple sometimes included in the dinners and cocktail parties that progressed up and down the street, making for a slightly unbalanced quintet of friends. Indeed, the Vollmers, who lived at the end of the Court, near the duck pond, had been taken up as something of a democratic experiment. Sarah Vollmer, childless and predisposed to costume jewelry and bright peasant weaves, was the only woman of the group who worked — beyond charity teas and chaperoning church-sponsored events. She taught dancing at the local high school sporadically, and one (meaning the regular Saturday golf foursome) could imagine her lithe body taut and then bending to the snap of castanets and a piano accompaniment. John Vollmer was also eccentric in his own way, for he owned a music store in the next town over. This slightly unconventional association with the arts was accentuated by the unconventional house they had built near the cul-de-sac at the end of the Court. Unlike the other structures of brick and frame and two-car garages along the street, this house was modern, with large glass widows staring into a long backyard and then the woods behind. It had only one level and no basement or attic. More than once and with some embarrassment, Celia Watson said of this arrangement that she could not imagine sleeping on the same level as the kitchen and dining room:

"There is something exotic, or is it erotic — is that the right word? — about a house with no upstairs and no privacy," she would say, reddening slightly. "It's like having a bathroom next to the dining room!"

Yet the group genuinely liked the Vollmers and often invited them, despite their lack of interest in golf or bridge or church. It made everyone feel warm with generosity to include this unusual couple and slightly experimental in their social relations to disrupt the normal even pairing that made their games possible.

Of the core group, Celia Watson was known to be high-strung and given to afternoon migraines, which she suffered in the dark of her bedroom, leaning against the soft satin headboard of her twin. She was thin, with sharp facial features and soft, straight blond hair that fell quickly out of any arrangement into its natural lank shape. Her husband, Steve, had never complained about her taste in frilly bedroom furniture, but Celia guessed his displeasure from his look of amazement and anguish on the day when the truck from Marshall Field's arrived and the two men tore off the wrappings to reveal the pleated pink material, puckered by white satin buttons. He said nothing and only contributed precise and strict orders for placing the furniture and then escaped quickly to the living room.

Together with the matching dressing table, laid out neatly with pots and bottles like a pharmaceutical display (creams and ointments and colorings of all shades), the bedroom furniture proclaimed loudly that this was her room and Steve, at best, was an interloper, tolerated — except, of course, when her migraine lasted into the evenings, as they frequently did. On such occasions, he retired to the study, a dark and friendly place, with a desk that he used only intermittently and a large, comfortable leather sofa, where he spent many nights. He had thought at one time of furnishing the room with a rack of rifles and a deer head, but seeing as he despised hunting, primarily for the cold and discomfort it occasioned, the room instead became a showcase for the single golf trophy he had won many years earlier and placed prominently on the mantel over the unused fireplace. Around this simple cup embossed with his name and a faintly etched golfer in midswing, he had placed various framed pictures taken during his business travels for the bank. All of them were similarly posed with the smiling, bland expressions of indistinguishable men in dark suits, their faces like white ivory buttons studding a black cardigan. The only oddity in this assemblage of images was a large, colorful map of Italy, where he had spent three years during the war. It was, despite its few touches of memory, truly his room. And he had spent enough nights there to earn possession of it. In fact, he had once thought of installing a daybed, but he didn't have the courage to face what he knew would be sharp looks of hurt from Celia.

Mornings were Celia's best time of the day, when Steve had gone off to work and about the time that the yellow school bus lumbered up and down Golf View, picking up children like the debris of past loves and escorting them for a full day at the local comprehensive school. Because the few Catholics in town sent their children to parochial school, the local grade school was effectively a Protestant mission that preached good manners and respect for adults as its gospel. Celia loved fall mornings, this being one, with nothing scheduled aside from shopping and a late afternoon trip to Miss Sandy's Hair Salon for her weekly perm. She was, therefore, pleased by a knock on the kitchen door and the appearance of Christine Barr from across the street.

Christine often joined her best friend for a second cup of morning coffee. The two sat like aging sorority sisters, Celia in her dressing gown with the white fake fur edging, and Christine with a coat thrown hastily over her shapeless morning dress. Both treasured these moments of intimacy and gossip — even if the subjects of their conversation rarely changed and they rehearsed the same sentiments and complaints.

This particular morning, however, Christine seemed anxious to move beyond the usual muddle of pleasantries. In fact, her ordinarily placid features were misshapen by anxiety, as if someone had yanked on her nerve endings, distorting her habitual smile and drawing the pudgy skin of her forehead together into fine furrows.

"I don't want to trouble you, Celia," she began after perching on the leatherette kitchen chair and gripping her hands around the coffee cup that had been placed in front of her.

"No, of course not. You aren't."

"But I've just come to the edge with Mr. Barr."

"Oh, dear," exclaimed Celia, knowing that when Christine used her husband's formal name, she was very angry. "It's not...?

"Yes, as a matter of fact, it is," interrupted Christine. "You know I've hinted at this before. And you as my best friend can surely see it."

"Yes, I do," replied Celia helpfully — but hoping that Christine would explain because she could not quite guess the source of her friend's unhappiness.

"It's his wandering eye. It's just so embarrassing! I know it doesn't mean anything. At least, I hope not. But last Sunday — you remember — we all had dinner together at the club."

"Yes, I do, and I remember you looked stressed and anxious."

"Well, I had good reason. You know I came a bit early and went out on the veranda to watch the golfers come in from the 18th hole. It was such a pleasant afternoon, and I wanted to enjoy the sun. I was sitting off to the side, and probably they didn't see me — our husbands, you know, walking off toward the locker room after paying off the caddies."

Celia wondered for a moment whether Christine had purposely hidden herself from view to engage the spectacle.

"And as usual, she — you know who I mean, I'm sure — was sitting right up front, smiling and chatting away with everyone like some kind of hostess. And dressed in those awful, revealing white shorts! Anyway, Teddy made a beeline for her and sat down at the table and ordered a drink. I just couldn't watch, and so I guess I sort of melted away. If Teddy saw me, it didn't register. Sometimes he can look right through me as if I weren't there."

Celia sat silently, but a feeling of intense sympathy, as well as worry, welled up inside her like coming tears.

"They just shouldn't let divorced women into the club. It's not right; it's too dangerous. I think men are difficult enough to handle without her being around."

"Oh, Christine! I am sorry," said Celia, stifling her emotion. "Men are just such prowlers, aren't they?" She said this with the utter confidence that Steve had never thought for a moment to stray. She felt intensely sorry for her friend, whether there was anything to the scene she recounted or not. And at the same time, she wondered what weakness in Christine, what flaw in her marriage, had made her become so suspicious. Perhaps, she thought, it was the money. Yes, her money — or rather, Daddy's dollars — for everyone thought (unkindly) that Christine had bought Teddy at auction when his golf career ended because of his injury.

"I know it's nothing," continued Christine, relaxing somewhat. "But one hears such stories. And divorce is such an awful thing to think about."

"But surely, you — that's not going to happen," Celia reassured her. And with this, she stood up and put her hand on Christine's shoulder. "I know just the thing. I have some chocolate cake left over from last night. It's a new recipe I tried out. Let's just indulge ourselves. It'll make you feel better."

"Oh, I shouldn't really," said Christine, squaring her shoulders and sitting straighter. "My figure, you know — it's such a struggle, and Teddy makes such a scene. But perhaps this once. A very small piece, then. You're the doctor."

Celia stood and walked over to the gleaming white Formica counter, which held a silver plastic cake stand. She removed the top, revealing a convex block of cut-open layer cake with alternating striae of cream and chocolate and smothered with chocolate icing as thick as turf. She reached above it to open the matching cabinet and took out two small plates. From the drawer below, she withdrew a wedge-shaped cake knife and measured off two small pieces. Christine watched this meticulous excavation as if it were the uncovering of a major archeological treasure.

"Really," she said to herself, "Celia overdoes it with her baking and her tidiness." Not, of course, that she herself was a slovenly and careless homemaker, although Teddy sometimes commented on a dinner that arrived in fits and starts as a result of mistiming and problematic calculations. And she never confessed the number of times a cake she had baked sagged and caved in upon itself like aging flesh as it cooled and had to be thrown in the trash. But, she reassured herself, one could be too neat and precise and too thin. And anyway, there was always the town bakery, where she was a devoted and frequent customer.

"This is really delicious," she found herself saying out loud. "You're a marvel, Celia!" She did not ask how Celia managed to remain so thin.

"It's nothing really. Just following a recipe. I could write it out for you if you like."

Christine was so intent upon taking small bites to make her piece last longer that she only looked up to smile. Teddy, of course, would love it if she mastered baking cakes; he enjoyed them. But she knew better than to eat sweets in front of him. Not, of course, that he ever said much out loud about her fluctuating weight; he was too polite or intimidated for that. Perhaps he remembered times when a chance remark set off a flood of angry tears and recriminations. No, it was the look he gave her, staring into her eyes with a warning that his next glance would fall on her ample stomach or her flabby upper arms. Was it, she wondered, his way of controlling her and asserting a measure of self-respect in a marriage where her money was a lopsided contribution? Whatever the reason, she knew that her sins of overeating could only be committed outside her own kitchen and dining room — in restaurants, where the presence of others would hush his criticisms, or privately with friends like Celia who happily urged her on.

"Another tiny sliver?" asked Celia obligingly, as if reading her thoughts. "I barely gave you any with the first piece."

Christine sucked in her stomach and smiled. "Only if you insist. And just a morsel."

As she said this, she wondered, somewhat cruelly, whether Celia was intentionally pushing the calories at her, tempting her in order to lessen the competition. Christine knew that even best friends could be jealous of each other, and the Golf View wives weren't beyond that sentiment.

How did she stay so thin? Christine wondered. Did Steve demand it? She wondered whether Celia's slight figure explained her hold on her husband. But even if Teddy encouraged her to diet and maintain her figure, she knew that other men were intrigued by the excesses of her figure. She could feel their probing eyes — Steve's included sometimes — almost pushing against her thighs and breasts, almost palpably following the curves of her torso. There were so many adjectives to describe her — ample, lusty, robust, pleasingly plump, bountiful, each a pleasant word. But all the synonyms of thin — and of Celia's slight figure — would be narrow, pinched and nasty. No, she wasn't jealous, she assured herself.

"Men!" she exclaimed suddenly.

"Oh, I do agree," said Celia, affirming that she understood, although she was quite puzzled, in fact, by her friend's non sequitur.

Chapter 2

That afternoon, after sleepwalking through her housework (rote tasks that she could, in fact, practically accomplish in her sleep), Christine sat clutching a cup of coffee on the back deck. Looking around her, she saw that grass was invading the seams of the brickwork like little tufts of annoyance. Someone would have to be put to work poisoning them. Although the day was neither warm nor cold, she shivered at the thought of another approaching winter. She stretched and sighed, looking out with vague interest at the messy garden plot, with its drooping cornflowers and heavy-headed hydrangeas, already turning brown with age. She knew she needed to ask one of the Clements boys to spend a Saturday clipping and mowing, because Teddy was generally hopeless, but even that was too much of an effort to contemplate. For now, she needed to relax. "Why," she asked herself, "am I so tired this afternoon? I can't even remember what I did today!"

Beyond the trees, she could catch the occasional glimpse of a golfer in pink or white shorts (it was Ladies' Day) and she wondered whether Mrs. Smith — Agnes Smith — was in one of the twosomes passing by. Really, she thought, they must do something about this menace; Celia had agreed, she thought. A widow who inherited her husband's membership in the club was one thing — and bad enough — but a divorcee who had demanded her husband's membership as part of her settlement was another thing entirely and so calculating. Certainly, she was a skilled golfer, probably with a lower handicap than many men and most of the wives who played, but it was the 19th hole where she dominated the course, dispensing smiles and, Christine thought, knowing glances at every overweight, sweating — and occasionally triumphant — male golfer who inevitably passed by her. Perhaps — as she convinced herself that a principle was involved — Marie Clements would know what to do. After all, Dan was a lawyer, and it would take something more than a spiteful look to dislodge Mrs. Smith from her siren's perch.

Christine stood up abruptly, with sudden determination, and re-entered the kitchen. She picked up the telephone receiver and juggled the switchhook several times until the familiar operator came on the line.

"Get me Marie Clements, will you please, Sally."

"Yes, Mrs. Barr. I'll ring her immediately."

After two rings, Marie answered.

"Hello, Marie. It's Christine."

Before she spoke again, Marie waited for the exit click of the operator.

"Hello, Christine, how are you?

"I'm fine," was the response, "but actually not so fine."

Marie, standing in her kitchen, put a hand on the counter as if to brace herself against the wave of emotion she could detect in Christine's voice. Why did she always call with some exaggerated slight or worry that bloomed like a drop of black ink in a bowl of clear water, and why just as she was trying to decide what outfit to wear for the evening? Dan was very particular that way, and she had learned early on that an ordinary dress or flat heels disheartened her husband, whose daily experience with women consisted of several secretaries who dressed in smart suits and crisp white blouses and nylons. He clearly expected the same or better at home, and she was happy to oblige.

"What's the problem?" said Marie guardedly, indicating her sympathy only cautiously enough to invite Christine to be brief.

"I've been thinking, and I happened to mention it also to Celia this morning, and while I was watching the golfers out back this afternoon, it came to me again. It's Ladies' Day, and so I was reminded twice of our problem at the club. You know what I think about the situation. I was hoping maybe you could bring it up to Dan. I know he's on the board of the Golf Association, and of course, he's a lawyer."

"You mean Mrs. Smith," said Marie, knowing full well Christine's preoccupation with the "Gay Divorcee," as the friends laughingly referred to her.

"I was just thinking it was time to act. Perhaps there can be a rule that divorcees can't be members. Or even single women or maybe some sort of half membership that would allow them to play but would require an escort to use the clubhouse or some sort of sponsor."

Marie stopped a laugh and then said more seriously:

"I doubt Mrs. Smith would ever lack for a sponsor or escort. That might just add to the problem."

Then, thinking better of her amusement at Christine's fixation, she added: "I do understand, though. But I doubt there's much we can do. I will talk to Dan tonight and get his thoughts on the matter. But right now, I have to run. My bath and then dress and pick Dan up at the station. We can certainly talk some more. Have you asked Jordan what she thinks? Maybe together we can all propose something. You know that the community has a responsibility to regulate itself, to maintain decorum and deal with threats."

"Decorum, yes — it's not a crusade," replied Christine, the hurt and discouragement impeding her voice as she imagined that Marie was dismissing her concern. "It just — well, never mind. Keep in touch. And one more thing: Is bridge still on for Friday?"

"Yes, of course. Why not?" Marie replied too quickly as she ran out of patience. She hung up abruptly, exhausted by Christine's emotion and anxiety, which seemed to transmit itself over the wire. She straightened her back and walked out of the kitchen to dress, pausing at the hall mirror in front of the stairway to attempt a smile, which, unfortunately, looked more like a grimace.

"Damn," she said softly. "If he sees me in this mood."

~~~

Jim Reilly was the first husband to arrive at the doorstep of his house on Golf View Court that evening. As he entered, he startled the small white terrier, Sam, who let out a half bark and howl and rushed over to nip at his ankle. Jim cried out in surprise and reached down to smack the perpetrator, who had already scampered away to a safe distance, wagging his tail ferociously. Jim thought that if dogs could laugh and set their faces in a grin of mockery, surely this mutt could.

"Jordan!" he called. "What the hell gives with that dog of yours? He has to know me by now."

Jordan entered the hallway from the staircase, two curlers still stuck in her hair and her shapeless muumuu unzipped in the back.

"You're early," she said, thinking that it was his fault that he had riled up the dog and, worse, caught her dressing.

"Obviously," he replied. "I waited to show a house over on the other side of town, but no one came. Can't trust a soul nowadays. So I thought, 'Why waste time at the office? Nothing ever happens on a Wednesday afternoon.' So here I am. You and your dog caught off guard. I wonder what I'd find if I came home even earlier."

"Jim Reilly," exclaimed Jordan, using his formal name in a mocking tone that she knew would wither his self-confidence. She understood this because she had watched his mother control his father's anger with just this put-down and knew that he hated the memory of it and the weakness it revealed.

"You shouldn't surprise Sammy," she continued. "He's still getting used to you."

"I should think by now he'd recognize the taste of my flesh," Jim countered. "Why don't you," he said, shifting gears into petulant overdrive, "bring me a whiskey, if you can tear yourself away from the mirror for a minute? Two ice cubes. I'll be in the den."

Jim leaned his empty briefcase against the leg of the hall table, and Sammy sneaked toward it, scraping his stomach on the ground, to investigate, as if it might be a hostile animal. Jim leaned down to pet the stiff hairs of the dog, but it cringed in fear.

"You and I have to call a truce," he said softly. "That is, if you want to stay. I know Jordan coddles you like a baby. Can't imagine holding a smelly dog like you in my arms. Just watch out, buster!"

Jim stood straight and muttered to himself. "Damned dog has got me talking to myself!"

As he walked through the hallway and then down two steps into the den, he pulled off his jacket, tossing it on the back of the leather chair, and then loosened his tie. He used both hands to smooth the thick brown hair that remained above his sideburns. He didn't need to consult a mirror to know that his face was ruddy and lined. Or that he already had dark stubble that etched shadows onto his cheeks. It made him, he thought, look slightly exotic, someone who would be noticed in a crowd. He had always played upon this impression by contrasting his slightly menacing look with an excess of jollity. It made him a good salesman and attractive to the women — who in the business of real estate, he had discovered, were the ones who made the crucial decisions about when and where to buy a house. And you could always squeeze a few more dollars out of them, he believed, if the approach was right. Selling a house was like conducting a public seduction.

Entering the room always improved his mood, because it was his room; and really, aside from the exclusive address, it was why he had insisted on this house. Jordan hadn't appreciated the location at first, fearing the isolation of a street with scarcely 10 houses on it, but Jim knew, as soon as he saw this room, that he had to have it. And anyway, lots of neighbors just meant lots of gossip, which he could well do without.

Naturally, he had changed the furnishings and, in fact, had a picture window installed, through which he could see the lawn and, beyond it, an extent of prairie grass and then the tree line of the golf course, just about where the strongest players hit their drives on the sixth hole. He had wanted to keep the wood paneling but ripped out several built-in bookshelves because he had no books to speak of, beyond the odd golf manual, a couple of textbooks that he kept from college and a few of his favorite novels. Anything else in print, besides Jordan's magazines, stayed in his office. All the furniture was heavy wood, upholstered with leather that had been softened like suede through use. In the corner opposite the window and across from his favorite adjustable lounge chair was the largest of the two television sets he owned, its round blank eye encased in a cabinet of dark wood. The other family television set sat in the living room, exclusively for Jordan to use. It was smaller and rested on a flimsy metal stand that was entirely incongruous with the decor of the room, which consisted of pastel-colored furniture covered in clear plastic to prevent wear. The plastic only came off for guests. There was also light blue wall-to-wall carpet, and there were busy flowered curtains, which Jordan had purchased upon the advice of the decorator she hired. Sitting in that room, he always felt that he was invading a model home meant only for show and designed for anything but comfort or conviviality. Even Jordan avoided it, except to watch the occasional afternoon soap opera. Instead, she spent most of her time in the kitchen or bedroom.

The den, in the original plan of the house, had been called a family room (he had looked at the plans prior to purchase), but with no family and only Sammy, whom Jim chased away every time he ventured onto the upper step, it had become his territory. And so the house was, in effect, divided into his and hers, with a gulf of silence separating two potentially hostile zones, like a "sitzkrieg" — he remembered the World War II term. Except, no, he thought, it wasn't exactly like that, for there were still a few moments of genuine accord. He sat down on his reclining leather chair, stretched out his legs and said out loud: "Just a bit melodramatic, aren't we?"

"What's melodramatic?" asked Jordan as she appeared on the landing of the den entrance, holding two etched whiskey glasses. She had removed the curlers from her hair and dressed in black velvet toreador pants and a tight white sweater. Her feet were shod in incongruous puffy pink raised-heel slippers. Sammy peered out from between her legs.

"Nothing. Just talking to myself," mumbled Jim. "How about that drink now?"

Jordan moved down the steps, her slippers scuffing audibly on the wood. Sammy followed closely behind. Jim, looking at the dog's face, imagined he almost detected a smirk — except that dogs don't smirk, he thought.

Jordan crossed the room and kissed his bare forehead so purposefully that it made him wonder whether the act was intended as mockery. As she stood up again, a rush of perfumed air washed over him.

"What's the drama about?" he asked.

"It's not drama," she said, backing away. "Just affection for my husband. And sorry about the dog. Really, you two should be friends. Perhaps if you tried..."

"Maybe you should talk to him first," Jim replied sarcastically. "But OK, I guess I'm just peeved about the client not showing up. I've been having trouble moving that house ever since it came on the market. It's just too small for this community. Really ought to tear it down. It's not a Clifton Terrace property, more like an outbuilding of some sort, and the houses around it are all larger. It just doesn't conform to the neighborhood, and so no one wants it. And you know the rule of fitting in for real estate."

He stopped to look at her intently for a moment, wondering whether the tight black pants were for him or for her.

"Come back over here for a moment," he said softly.

"Oh, not now, Jim, not now! What were you thinking? I have to get dinner ready." She retreated quickly back up the steps, clutching her drink, Sammy just a half-step behind, although when he reached the landing, he turned back to glare at Jim.

"Dogs and women!" Jim said to himself, and then he chuckled. "I'm like a character in 'A Thurber Carnival.' What's the name of that story, 'The Dog That Hated People'? No, 'That Bit People.' That's it. I'll have to read it again sometime."

He took a long, slow drink of his whiskey, which burned pleasantly in his throat as he swallowed. In a few minutes, he would feel the first warm blur that would wipe out the rest of the evening.

~~~

Marie Clements parked her cream and red Buick Roadmaster convertible (with the white canvas top up) about a block below the exit to the commuter rail station in the tiny downtown area of Potawatomi Acres. She was early and could have moved up considerably, seeing as the line of waiting wives had not yet filled in, but she always chose this spot. There was no particular reason except that she had learned, from watching her husband walk down the slight hill, to gauge his mood from his stride. There was no single gesture that spoke to her, and she could never really articulate exactly the measure she used; perhaps it was the speed of his gait or whether he slapped his thigh with his folded Sun-Times or whether he squared his shoulders or he slouched when he saw the car. But she could just about predict what the evening would be like from his amble.

After the train arrived, she watched as the first men began to stream out of the station. Dan was never first because he got onto the back of the train at LaSalle Street, where he met three other lawyers from town for a hasty round of bridge played across adjoining seats. In an odd arrangement, the train cars had reversible seats so that the train wouldn't have to be turned around in order for passengers to be able to face forward, and if Dan and his friends could find two empty rows, they could reverse one and the teams could face each other.

Today, as Marie glimpsed Dan's heavy figure coming down the hill, briefcase in hand, he had a bounce in his step, as if the sidewalk had a spring in it. She thought to herself, "It will be a good evening." She slid across the white leather seat to the passenger side and waited.

"Hello," he said as he opened the heavy door and eased himself under the steering wheel. He put his case between them but leaned over to kiss her on the cheek.

"Top not down? It's pretty nice weather," he said.

"Well, I would have, but I just had my hair done, and the wind would have devastated it." Unconsciously, she touched the bottom of her stiffly permed hair, which glistened like a tarnished gold helmet in the slanting rays of the fading sun.

"Looks nice," he said without looking, and he reached down to the steering column to start the car.

He twisted the key, and once the motor caught, he gunned the engine. It was his favorite moment of the day, when he felt the power surge of eight thrusting pistons and the vibration of the Buick before it settled into gear. He looked briefly at Marie, admiringly, not because he realized that she was an actual beauty. But he was as proud of her as he was of his powerful automobile. They were his most prized possessions.

He guided the Buick through the railroad underpass and then roared up to the only stoplight in town, which had just turned red.

"Dan!" exclaimed Marie. "Slow down. You'll kill somebody!"

He turned to look at her with a blank, disapproving look, purposely ignoring her warning.

"How are the boys?" he asked. "Not into any trouble today, I hope?"

"No, it's only a school night," she replied. "They were fine when I left. I told them not to stray. I think Edgar has a math test tomorrow. I told him you'd help him out. I guess he takes after me. I never did have a mind for figures; not like you."

"Sure, I'll help. I have to go over a brief, but I can find time if he can."

"I'll make sure," she said, thinking to herself that the little discipline administered to her sons inevitably came from her. Dan was her fallback, her moral authority, but she knew that when he had to intervene, he put on his worst lawyer know-it-all voice, which made her instantly sympathize with the culprit.

When the light turned green, Dan pressed his foot heavily on the gas, and the car lurched forward, spitting gravel from the rear wheels.

"I don't want to say anything," Marie began.

"Then don't. It just makes me relax to feel all that energy. Anyway, what is all the horsepower for if you can't use it?"

"Well, just don't let the boys see you do that. You know that Dan Jr. is about to take his driver's test, and we've had enough trouble already with Edgar running off and drinking with his buddies." She looked ahead staring blankly at the road, studying the street she had driven over hundreds of times.

"God, it makes me feel old to think of the boys growing up!" she said.

"Don't start, Marie. You aren't old, and you certainly don't look old. I've got all the bills — the hairdresser, the salon, Marshall Field's, the manicurist, the druggist — to prove that you're still looking young, or at least working very hard at it."

"It's all for you, Dan."

"Maybe," he said suspiciously. "But sometimes I think it's not. Just for the other bridge club ladies. You certainly dress up better for them than you do for me."

"But that's going out for a social occasion. I'd die if I thought my friends believed I was letting myself go. You don't understand. When you play golf with your foursome, I know you wear your rattiest old clothes. You just don't care; but I have to."

"It's to be comfortable. And if I showed up in golf knickers and a pastel Lacoste shirt, they'd hoot me off the links. No, guys don't dress for each other."

"Perhaps not," said Marie, suddenly brightening to her insight. "But perhaps you actually do dress for 'the guys' in a way. Look at that closetful of business suits you own. I hope that isn't to charm your secretaries. And then, isn't dressing down just the same as dressing up if you're trying to make an impression of not caring?"

Dan looked at her skeptically and then turned back to focus on the road. He said nothing as he braked to head into Golf View. Slowing past the first house on the block, he pulled in to the driveway of No. 209 and edged up alongside Marie's small Nash Rambler. He had purchased automatic Powerglide — or whatever it was called — for her because she was forever grinding the gears of the Buick, trying to use the stick shift. That was why he rarely let her drive it. But he had taught both his sons to drive a car with a standard transmission. If you couldn't use a clutch, he always said, you couldn't really control a vehicle. He had stressed that fact over and over to Edgar and then Dan Jr.; it was probably the most important lesson a father could impart to a son.

Stopping the car up against the garage, he turned off the engine and reached for his briefcase. He swung the heavy door wide and slid out, allowing it to close with a satisfying clunk of metal on metal. Walking toward the side entrance of the house, he entered without looking back. Marie sat for a moment, watching his movements. She had seen him do this a thousand times over — so many times that he had probably forgotten that once, much earlier in their relationship, he would have walked around to open the car door for her. She was sure that he would not even remember such transitory rituals of courtship, but she hadn't forgotten. Sighing, she pushed open the door and swung her legs out. Walking to the door, she could hear voices inside, a murmur of words that she had no interest whatsoever in distinguishing. She continued up the steps and into the hallway that led to the kitchen. When she opened the swinging door into the room, she felt an immediate wave of depression. The breakfast and lunch dishes were still stacked in the sink like the abandoned artillery pieces of a routed army. And she hadn't even begun to think about dinner. Not planning anything meant a quick tuna casserole. She knew she had several tins of fish in the cupboard but walked over just to be sure. Yes, Chicken of the Sea and plenty of macaroni shells. She could make breadcrumbs to cover it and then toss a salad. It might take a while, and Edgar was sure to complain again. But what else could she do? Where had the day gone? she wondered.

~~~

Just as Marie finally served dinner to her sullen family, quieted by hunger and boredom, Celia Watson had finished washing the dishes and taken her wine glass into the living room, where Steve had dug himself into the evening paper. She sat down on the couch across from her husband and distracted herself for a moment, trying to read the upside-down headlines of his folded paper. He didn't look up at her, so she cleared her throat in the habitually angular, resonant pitch that announced her need for attention.

"Steve," she began.

He made a gruff noise of acknowledgment but kept the paper at eye level.

"I've been thinking about the club," she continued.

He turned the page and grunted again.

"I think there's a serious problem."

Interested now, he put down his reading and looked at her intently.

"I talked to Christine today, and she's extremely worried. And now I am, too. I think we really need to do something about her."

"Christine?" asked Steve, puzzled.

"No, of course not. We both agree. It's that woman with the blond hair. What's her name? Smith, Agnes Smith, I think. Well, anyway, you're on the board. Can't you do something about her? I mean, she's not even a member in her own right; just handed it by some judge. You ought to pass a resolution: No widows or divorcees."

Steve looked at her with amazement. "You want me to do what? Cancel her membership somehow? But why? I can think of a dozen reasons not to, beginning with the fact that it's plainly illegal. And anyway, who cares?"

"Well, I care; Christine cares even more, and I imagine every other wife who's seen her in action cares. And that means you should care, too."

"Not possible," Steve said, picking up his paper and rattling it as if to punctuate the end of a conversation. "And from what I understand," he added suddenly, "she and her ex-husband were very good friends with the club manager. She probably still is. Might not pay to interfere." She gave up for the moment but determined she would try again.

~~~

By 10 that evening, Christine and Teddy sat in the living room watching the television news. Christine still held her book in her lap, a finger to mark the place she had left off reading. Teddy was only half-listening because nothing interested him except the weather report. He had his usual foursome planned for Saturday or Sunday, whichever day held the best prospects in this changeable season. The worst problem would be wind, so common in fall, which could sweep down and carry a perfect drive into the rough. When he heard that both days would be clear and cool, he stood to switch off the set.

"I guess that does it for tonight," he concluded. Christine looked at him as he straightened from a slouch and wondered why he always insisted on controlling the television set when he was home. He was still a good-looking man, although of late, a paunch had begun to spill over his belt like an edge of soft risen bread dough on the lip of a bowl. He still had the remnants of the dark good looks that had once intrigued her, although as she studied his face, she noted that his eyebrows were flecked with white. As he turned to go upstairs, he reached down to massage the thigh of his right leg, tending almost unconsciously to the injury that had ruined his professional golf career.

"So you'll get at least one good round in," she said encouragingly, "whichever day you play. We can all have supper at the club. We don't have any other plans this weekend."

Teddy reached over to turn out the lamp next to her chair, but she said sharply, "Leave it. I'm still reading. I'll be up later."

He looked at her and then reached out with his hand and placed it on her shoulder, squeezing gently. She stiffened at this familiar signal.

"I'd like for you to come to bed now," he said.

"Oh, you go on ahead," she insisted. "I'll be along. I'm not really tired, and this is such an interesting book. It's all about modern psychology. I just never imagined."

"You don't have to be exhausted to come to bed, you know," replied Teddy with a hopeless whine.

"Oh, don't I know that!" said Christine. "It's just that tonight, well, not tonight. I'd never fall asleep."

"OK then, Christine, I'm going upstairs. I'll lock up first."

He turned and walked out of the room. In the distance, she could hear his step and then a heavy clunk as he turned the deadbolt on the front door. If such sounds could convey disappointment or even anger, she thought she detected it. She had actually anticipated that with Sandy off at school, she and Teddy might become closer. She had convinced herself that having a teenage daughter in an adjoining bedroom had somehow inhibited her. But despite Sandy's room being empty now, nothing had changed. In fact, she and Teddy had drifted even further apart than ever, and she realized that she just didn't always want him, at least not so often as he made one of those absurd gestures that in his mind passed for romance. It was too much of a bother. Easy enough for him; just roll on and roll off. But for her, the chemistry (as she called it) was so much more complex. A squeeze of her shoulder — his usual signal — or even sometimes a placing of his hand on her breasts inside her nightgown was only an annoyance, and she would shudder instead of shiver. She had lost the ability to tingle. No longer would her skin blaze. No longer would every sensation during intimacy be like a confusion of intense pleasure and pain. What had happened to them? she asked herself. How had excitement become habit and then duty and then indifference?

She waited several more minutes until she thought he would be asleep, and then she looked down at her book. She was still on the same page; she had been reading the same paragraph again and again without realizing it. She dog-eared her place, closed the book and placed it on the table next to the lamp. She switched off the light and then moved mechanically through the darkened room toward the hallway and the stairs. It seemed to her that the house was still strangely alive with reflected light, from the street lamp in front and perhaps the upstairs night light in the hall, just giving shape to objects, not any color, as if all the bright shades of the interior had now been dulled to a tarnished brass. The color of her life? she mused. She made her way slowly up the stairs, realizing suddenly that she was tired after all.

Chapter 3

It was Marie Clements' turn on Friday to host the afternoon bridge game on the eve of their husbands' golf match. Ever since the Barrs had moved onto the street two years earlier and completed the quartet of friends, this had become an unbroken ritual every other week. The game progressed up and down Golf View, and on this particular afternoon, Celia Watson's Chevrolet and Christine Barr's Cadillac were parked in the driveway behind the two-tone Buick. Jordan, of course, had walked — merely across the street. The Clements boys had raked leaves the night before and polished the Buick convertible. They were not expected home until about 4 o'clock and had strict instructions to come in quietly and retire to their rooms. Of course, they were also expected to say hello if the game was still on, but they were to leave immediately.

Just as the party moved up and down the block in regular order, so the food offered at each gathering was chosen, as if by an invisible hand, from the latest recipes in Ladies' Home Journal and Redbook. Quivering green and red Jell-O molds filled with suspended chunks of fruit, flourless chocolate cakes, whole-wheat crumpets once (a decided failure), cookies with walnut clusters and teas and coffees were the revolving afternoon fare. If there was an element of competition to this provisioning, none of the women would own up to it except, after receiving the expected praise, to confess that she was trying out a new recipe to please Teddy or Dan or Steve or Jim later.

Just as these offerings contained a muted striving for superiority designed to elicit praise from the group, so each member dressed for the others in a way to attract a compliment or even incite envy. Of course, Jordan could do nothing to disguise her desire to be the first among equals in fashion and spent several hours after a light, early lunch on Fridays bathing, powdering herself and sitting in her favorite satin slip in front of the tri-fold vanity mirror, embellishing her features with subtle touches of shadow and bright red.

Christine always put off dressing until the last moment, knowing that when she rummaged through her wardrobe looking for the perfect outfit, she was likely to run across some older garment that was now too tight in the buttocks or waist. She wanted no reminder, especially on a day when she intentionally discarded all thoughts of dieting, that remaining slim was a struggle to regain her former self, the one she knew to be the truest — the girl who had driven Teddy wild with desire. No, on such afternoons, she looked at herself in the full-length mirror attached to the inside door of her closet and, seeing the almost Rubens-esque figure that she had become, wondered why, if other men still stared at her with lust, Teddy had become the mess sergeant of her life, watching over her dinners and doling out, when they ate together, increasingly stingy portions. So she usually picked a white blouse and dark skirt that emphasized her large figure. It was almost an act of defiance to unbutton two notches down to reveal the deep shadow of her enviable chest. She reached across to her open perfume bottle and tipped a drop onto her index finger, which she then dabbed onto the skin between her breasts.

Celia tried valiantly on these occasions to dress smartly but only succeeded in making the wrong choices, for the clothes she bought were those that she wanted to be able to wear but never quite fit her narrow hips and pinched shoulders. Christine had once said (unkindly) that the silk dress she was wearing made her look like a limp flag waving in surrender. This unthoughtful remark had stood between the two neighbors like a broken truce for weeks until, by careful increments of compliments, Christine had renewed their alliance and Celia forgave her. Yet the memory of this remark often came back in the form of an uneasy feeling, an exasperation that mounted as she tried on one outfit after another, finally choosing something that was a compromise between ill-fitting and bad taste.

As for Marie, dressing was never really a problem but rather an opportunity to model her latest acquisition from

Field's or Bonwit Teller. It was not, she told herself, an attempt to advertise her enormous clothing budget but rather an effort to try out her latest purchases in front of a critical and appreciative audience before she modeled them for Dan. Given their Chicago connections, through Dan's downtown law partnership, she felt she had to dress the role. It angered her sometimes to think that she was isolated here in Potawatomi Acres, a golf mecca 50 miles from the elegant estates of Dan's law partners in Lake Forest and Winnetka in this backwater of tidy lawns and three-bedroom brick colonials, but he had insisted that they live as close to his great passion as possible. She sometimes thought that if they had moved to the North Side and lived in a different world, perhaps his passion might have been redirected more in her direction or toward the exciting cultural events that she imagined preoccupied life along the North Shore. But there was no knowing.

With the foursome united inside Marie's comfortable living room and the card table set up in the middle, after a brief round of compliments, the women quickly assumed their places. Just for these occasions, Marie had purchased matching chairs and a black Naugahyde surface to play on. As usual, the thick shag rug made the table slightly wobbly, but not enough to upset their drinks or the ashtray that sat next to Marie's place. (Marie had offered martinis all around, although Celia, as usual, protested that she could only drink half.) Christine had chosen the chair that allowed her to gaze occasionally into the dining room alcove to glimpse the preparations for their midgame break. She could see several bottles of gin and vermouth and an ice bucket and beyond, in a corner of the table, the tantalizing vision of a white frosted cake, no doubt purchased from her favorite bakery, she told herself. (Marie hadn't the patience or talent to bake.) So she sat back, reassured that the afternoon would be a pleasant one. And her partner today would be Jordan, the most accomplished player of them all.

Marie's living room was brightened by the afternoon sun streaming through the oversize picture window that looked west. The heavy taffeta curtains and overhanging valance framed the glass as if setting the stage for a domestic drama. The whole room, in fact, was aglow in reflected colors. The pale green walls seemed almost white with the intense glare of the outside light, and the matching flowered furniture covers flushed with intensity, making the room faintly reminiscent of a flower garden. As the women settled in, Marie produced a fresh package of Kent cigarettes, pulling off the crackling cellophane wrapper to reveal a perfect row of filter tips looking like gleaming canine teeth. She set it alongside a large brass lighter in the shape of a genie's lamp.

"I've decided to switch brands," she said casually, pulling open the hinged cardboard to reveal a bouquet of white filters. "There are so many new brands to choose from now," she continued, "but I like these best. There's something elegant about them, don't you think? And they are supposed to be for us, for women." She demonstrated by picking out one to hold delicately between her first and second fingers.

"I'd certainly like to try one," said Celia cautiously, "but Steve doesn't like it if I smoke. He says it leaves a smell in my hair — not that he ever gets close enough to tell." She intended this as a joke and managed a brief smile, but it only sounded to the others like bitterness.

"Then, by all means, you must have one," said Jordan with a grimace that lapsed into a fleeting scowl.

There was a brief moment of silence as Celia tentatively reached into the pack and extracted a slender cigarette. She picked up the heavy lighter and flicked the small ribbed wheel with her thumb several times. A tiny blue flame finally shot up and caught the end of her cigarette. She inhaled deeply.

"That's very nice," she said to the other women, who had been watching her keenly.

Marie then produced a pad of paper and a new deck of cards, which she placed at the center of the table.

"I think, if I remember correctly, it's your turn to score," she said to Christine. "We can give you a minute to set things up." She opened the box containing the cards and, with a skillful thrust, flicked through the pack, bending and separating the cards with an audible flutter.

"I love the design, don't you?" she said, spreading the cards in a half-moon across the table.

"The backs are an art nouveau design. Something I picked up downtown. And the faces — well you can see how wonderfully drawn they are, almost antique in style."

"They're lovely!" exclaimed Christine as she picked up a card and turned it over to look at the elegant queen of diamonds. "It reminds me of a painting."

"Yes, it's supposed to," said Marie, pleased that her purchase had elicited admiration. "But shall we begin? We can cut the deck to see which pair leads off." She reassembled the deck and held it out to Jordan. "You first, and then Celia. Highest card begins."

Jordan reached for the deck, divided it almost in the middle and turned up the pile in her hand. It was an ace. Celia, with a discouraged look on her face, exclaimed, "I'll concede. I can't match that! Oh, I hope it won't be one of those days!"

"Lucky at cards!" Jordan said, picking up the deck.

"If only," Celia replied defiantly, reaching for her cigarette.

The game went quickly, in part because all four players concentrated on winning. Gradually, the room became heavy with the scent of perfume and cigarette smoke. During what proved to be the deciding game of the first rubber, Celia, who was sitting out because Marie had won the bid, suddenly said: "I've been meaning to say something all afternoon, and I hope it won't distract from the game, but I just read a very disturbing article. I think it was in Redbook or maybe the Journal."

Marie looked over her cards and across the table at her partner quizzically.

"You suddenly look just awful, Celia. What is it? Shouldn't we play this hand out and then we can talk about it?"

"Yes, of course," said Celia. "I'm sorry to interrupt."

"What is the matter?" asked Christine timidly, her curiosity drawing a reproachful glance from Jordan, who wanted to play through what she thought was a winning hand.

"Just an article I read in the doctor's office two days ago. But please, finish the game, and then I'll tell you. I'm sorry I just blurted it out."

The remaining few tricks were taken in silence, and then Marie said, "Let's have some refreshments, and then you can reveal your mystery, Celia."

The four women got up and walked into the dining room, where they helped themselves to cake and more drinks. When they had returned to the bridge table, Celia looked at her friends carefully. It was rare that she could command their full attention, but something in the quality of her voice, an insistence and urgency, had intrigued them. Even Christine seemed distracted from enjoying the cake in front of her.

"I was in Dr. Brewer's office two days ago for a minor complaint," Celia began. "You know how long you have to wait sometimes. Well, I just got bored, and so I picked up a magazine." She stopped to make sure that she still held their attention, because she intended, just this once, to draw out her story. "Anyway, I was looking through it, mainly for recipes. I've told you how picky Steve can be when it comes to dinner. I've tried everything and was hoping for a new way to make pot roast." She stopped, but instead of a dramatic pause in the narrative, this hiatus in her story was an excuse for Marie to stand.

"I think I'll put the coffee on. You can finish telling us later, Celia."

"No, no, really, please wait just a minute. I'll hurry up, because I really also want your advice."

Reluctantly, Marie sank back down in her seat with a look of exasperation, as if the story would never end.

"I was paging through, and I happened on an article by some doctor and somebody else. I doubt I can recall their names, but I do remember that they worked at Johns Hopkins Hospital in Baltimore. Anyway, the title — and I could never forget it because it was such a shock — the title was 'Frigidity in Women.'"

Celia immediately blushed and put one hand to her face as if to hide her embarrassment.

"Such an awful idea. And I could scarcely read through it to the end. It was utterly shocking!"

Before she could continue, Christine interrupted: "I think we all need another piece of cake. At least I do!" She stood abruptly and put her hand sympathetically on Celia's shoulder. Looking at Jordan, she saw that her face was twisted into a wry smile as if Celia had suddenly revealed a deep and damaging secret about herself. She looked up at Christine as if to say, "I knew it all along."

But Celia remained seated at the table, her discomfiture spreading across her face, discoloring it in blotches like a wine stain on a white carpet. On seeing this distress, Christine sat down again.

"And I feel awful about what I did," continued Celia. "I've never acted like this in my life, but I knew I couldn't just go out and buy the magazine. What if Steve saw it?

What would he think about me? And so I did something I shouldn't have. I slipped the magazine into my purse and then went to the ladies' room and locked myself in a cubicle. No one came in while I was there. So I ripped the pages out and then went back into the waiting room and put the magazine back. And I have the article here."

She reached down beside her and picked up her baby blue plastic handbag, put it in her lap and snapped it open. Pulling out several folded sheets, she opened them and began to read in a trembling voice, struggling through the dry prose:

"'An Old Problem With a New Name.' That's the title. Here's what it says: 'The frigid housewife may be defined as a woman who experiences pain or anxiety during intercourse and who never achieves the physical or emotive heights of satisfaction that are possible but rather looks at the sex act as a duty at best or, worse, with disgust and guilt. This condition...'" Celia hesitated as she skipped a paragraph or two to get to the main point. "'This common condition,'" she resumed, "'which strikes one marriage in three, is, in fact, the result of multiple causes acting in concert or alone.'"

Celia stopped to catch her breath.

"'In a very few cases,'" she continued firmly, "'this problem is entirely physical in origin and in the most extreme instances may result from misshapen or injured sexual organs. Much more often, however, it is a psychological problem which prevents the woman from achieving a full and deep release, whether this stems from some lingering childhood memories that haunt the marital bedroom, a feeling of reluctance, inadequacy and embarrassment, an ignorance of physiology or, what is most likely, a lack of interest in or understanding of the husband's needs. Regardless of the cause, however, this disability is a major impediment to marital bliss and may well necessitate the intervention of a medical doctor or psychologist. If left untreated, it often leads to divorce.'"

"'Our reporters interviewed Dr. Irwin A. Blatchford of the Psychiatric Institute of the Johns Hopkins University School of Medicine. Frigid women...' I just can't go on," exclaimed Celia. "But you see, don't you?"

No one said a word for a minute as they watched Celia intently. Jordan thought to herself that the description must fit Celia perfectly, or else she wouldn't have been so shocked by reading it. There was, Jordan had always noticed, something brittle about her friend, a snappishness and tendency to inappropriate and exaggerated emotion. She went from enthusiasm to despair and back again too easily. It must be, she concluded, hell to live with someone like that, whose moods were so unpredictable. Jordan knew that she, of course, wasn't frigid and that if she didn't really enjoy sex very much with Jim anymore (she secretly called him "hasty Jim"), this was just the natural declension of marriage. Men liked the act more than women, and anyway, as one aged... But it was nothing to be clinical about.

Jordan stopped her thought because she realized that she had spoken the last words out loud.

"What was that?" Marie asked. "Did you say something, Jordan?"

"Yes, actually, I was thinking that it was such a clinical description and so impersonal and cold. I'm not sure it's very helpful to print such stories. They can disturb the impressionable. And I certainly don't think it's true. I'd really like to see the same attention paid to men — just for once. I think we all enjoy sex. I know I do. I just wish there was more romance occasionally."

"But," said Celia, tears beginning to glaze her eyes, "if it's a real problem, don't you think we should know about it? I mean, what if I'm frigid? I know it's a terrible thing to say about oneself, but I can't help myself thinking about it. Ever since we gave up trying to have children, Steve and I — I think I can tell you — we just don't do it much anymore. It's just a bother, and if it isn't just right, he gets mad at me and sulks, and that makes it worse. I try. I really do. But sometimes it's so sudden, so unexpected when he wants to that I'm just not ready or I'm tired or I have a headache. I mean, men are so inconsiderate."

She stopped and wiped one eye with the corner of her paper napkin.

"I shouldn't have said any of this, I know. But you're my friends."

Marie stood and put her hand on Celia's shoulder.

"Let's finish our cake, and I'll serve some coffee. I'm not sure we need to resume the game, though. Maybe this is something we need to discuss further. I agree that what Celia read is very disturbing, and I, for one, share her feeling that this could be a problem, although I have no idea what to do about it. At the least, if doctors are talking about it, it must be a problem."

Jordan also stood and walked resolutely into the dining alcove.

"Well, I'm going to have another piece of this delicious cake and another martini," she said, turning back, "if we are going to talk about this. It's nothing to discuss on a half-empty stomach, and anyway, I don't think I can be entirely honest if I'm sober and have a clear head. Inhibitions, you know." Laughing, she descended upon the table and took the silver cake knife in her hand. Looking back at the bridge table, she exclaimed:

"I think we should all fortify ourselves."

Marie looked bemused at her friend, for this was, she thought, so like Jordan to try to take over and dominate. It often made her wonder whether in her relationship with Jim she was as assertive.

"And," said Celia, standing and walking toward the dining room, "there's also the problem of that terrible Mrs. Smith, who Christine and I have been discussing. I just think all of this is somehow related."

Christine raised her eyebrows in a secret gesture of exasperation. She had said her piece about Mrs. Smith and realized nothing could be done. But Celia, once her wind blew her in a certain direction, could not be diverted. So be it, she said to herself. They might as well talk about everything, and perhaps, just maybe, it was all of a piece.

Marie, who had disappeared into the kitchen for a minute, called from the dining room. "There's coffee now."

The other three women walked into the room and served themselves.

"If everyone has what they want, let's go back to the card table for a moment," said Marie. "I think we've had enough bridge for today, and I can see that you're upset, Celia. You're shaking so much I think you'll spill your coffee. Let me carry it in for you," she commanded.

Celia relinquished her cup and saucer, and the group moved back to the bridge table and sat down. Marie returned to the dining room for a moment and then came back with a whiskey glass containing three perfect cubes of ice, filled almost to the brim, and set it down in front of Celia.

"Drink up," she ordered.

"But Steve — he'll know, and I'll be so tipsy I won't be able to make dinner. I'll have to lie down."

"Sometimes that just happens," said Marie forcefully. "Sometimes you just can't be the perfect housewife, and anyway, I'll be sure to shoo you all out of the front door by 5 o'clock. Dan expects me at the station."

"Look who's the brave one now," said Jordan to herself, glaring at Marie.

Christine ate her cake slowly to savor the sweet, creamy icing. But somehow this indulgence did not overcome the nasty flavor of the article that Celia had read.

"I think it's all very disturbing," she began. "I've heard that term 'frigid' somewhere before. Perhaps I saw it in a magazine, too. But I just don't believe it. I know I'm not like that, and I really doubt if you are, either, Celia." She brightened as if struck by an unexpected thought.

"What if it's the men at fault?" she began tentatively. "What if they just don't understand us? After all, it's mostly male doctors and male psychologists, isn't it, who come up with these ideas? And of course, the author of that article is a man, too, isn't he?"

Celia put her glass down and pulled out the sheet again.

"It's actually two writers," she said after glancing at it. "A man and a woman, I think, who helped out."

"Yes, no doubt," continued Christine. "One to give it a point of view and shape the argument and the other to do all the work and put it into reasonable prose. And we can guess which is which."

She broke off, seeing that she now had their complete attention.

"I'm going to say only one thing about the article, not that I've read it. No need for all of us to let down our hair, but I will tell you that sometimes Teddy gives me a wry look and touches me on the shoulder and then he expects that that turns on the electricity and that I'll sparkle and crackle like a live wire. Well, no, it just doesn't work that way. Men forget that before marriage, they had to show affection, court us with flowers and compliments and gifts, and open doors for us. And now it's just, 'Hey, honey, let's do it' — as if they had the guts to actually say something as rude as that. So they think up some cute little signal instead!"

The other three women looked momentarily shocked at Christine's frankness, but she could sense their assent given, almost unconsciously.

Jordan was the first to break the silence. "I suppose you have a point," she said in a neutral voice. But she would never admit to anyone, least of all her friends, that Jim sometimes, on the infrequent occasions when they made love, had his own private repertoire of gestures to which she was expected to respond. But she did not allow herself to say anything. Instead, she asked:

"Where do you suppose they learn this behavior? Do you suppose they talk about it in the locker room? At sports events? I just can't imagine. My guess is that they are so stunted emotionally that all they can do is tell jokes to cover their embarrassment and ignorance. Where the hell is the passion?"

There was another silence that suddenly seized them, as if the dying afternoon sun had drawn off the energy from the room. The murky gauze of twilight darkened the walls and furniture, and Marie, suddenly aware of the gloom, stood as if to turn on the lights. But before she could do so, a voice from the entrance hall called out:

"Mom, what are you all doing sitting in the dark? Playing bridge still? How can you see the cards?" said Edgar as he walked into the room. "Do you mind if I switch on the lights?" he asked as he clicked on the overhead recessed spotlights, which restored pools of diffused color to the rug and walls.

"Come in and say hello," Marie said, recovering her sense of command. "And where is Dan Jr.?" She stood and walked to the two lamps that bordered the large flowered couch and turned them on. The starkness of the overhead spots immediately dissolved.

"Oh, he's outside putting away his bike in the garage. Hello, everyone," he continued, nodding at the three women still seated at the bridge table. And then he quickly withdrew from the room.

"Such a polite boy, Marie," said Christine as she stood again, smoothing her skirt. "But I think I'll leave now. I didn't realize the hour."

She looked at Celia, who still sat in her chair, diminished, as if she had suddenly been compressed into old age. Even her bland, stringy hair seemed to have thinned and flattened against her scalp.

"Yes," said Jordan. "Come along, Celia. And we certainly thank you, Marie. As always, a lovely time."

Celia stood suddenly and shook off the apparition that had weighed on her.

"I'm sorry to have been so down in the dumps. I somehow feel reassured now that I told you about the article. And I appreciate your confidence. Is that the word?"

Marie looked at Celia in disbelief because confidence was the last thing they had bestowed on her. Perhaps there had been a moment of confiding, yes, and there were secrets that even the best of friends would keep so close that they passed into deniability, but she guessed no one was feeling self-confident. She would be pleased when her guests were gone and she could clean up before she had to fetch Dan at the station. She knew he would be full of complaints once he realized that the revolving bridge game had taken place in his living room. He always remarked on the traces of smoke and perfume as if they had transformed his house into a public space and not his comfortable domain. She knew he would comment and then ask, in a voice that anticipated offense, whether they would have a regular dinner, which meant, according to him, she imagined, one she had spent hours making in the kitchen. Well, perhaps she could disguise some leftovers as a new dish, a stew perhaps of pieces of steak and some vegetables from last night. At least then when he complained, she could give him a condescending smile and confess, with much feigned shame, "Yes, I just had time to throw something together. The bridge club stayed later than usual." If he wanted to complain, let him!

Edgar watched the three women exit the house from the open garage, where he had joined Dan Jr., who was fiddling with the hand brakes on his bicycle. He shook his head slowly and said out loud, "Grown-ups and their games!"

Christine paused by the side of her car, kissed her hand and waved at Jordan as she crossed the street and then flung open the door of the Cadillac. She sat for a moment fidgeting with the key, until the engine roared to life like some wild beast shocked from sleep. Glancing briefly into the rearview mirror, she punched the shift into reverse and lurched out of the driveway into the street. Without stopping, she changed into drive and sped off, too quickly, because her abrupt change of gears drew an angry growl and then a clunk from the car's Hydramatic drive. Celia, who had parked next to her, crawled out in her wake.

"They drive like teenagers," laughed Dan Jr., pointing at the street with a wrench that he held in his greasy hand.

"Or worse," chimed in his brother. "I guess we should go in now and help Mom set the table, before we're called. You coming?"

"Yeah, just give me a minute. Soon as I tighten this brake. You know what's for dinner?"

"Don't have a clue except that it's bridge night, and that could mean anything or nothing."

"Not looking forward to seeing Dad's face, then."

"I never am," said Edgar as he turned to walk out of the garage.

At about 9 that evening, when Christine was sure that Teddy had retired permanently to his den, she telephoned Jordan. The phone rang several times, and she was about to hang up, when Jordan finally came on the line.

"You're out of breath," she said.

"Oh, hello, Christine. Yes, I was outside just for a minute with the dog when the phone rang.

"Well, if you're busy, we can talk later."

"Not at all."

"It's just that this afternoon was terribly disturbing. I mean Celia. Don't you think? And I know that Marie was also upset. I wanted to talk about it."

"I don't know, actually," replied Jordan slowly. "I don't believe that article one bit. Celia's just grasping at straws, trying to understand why Steve has stopped paying attention to her. I'll bet she thinks that something is happening with Mrs. Smith at the club. I wish you hadn't suggested it. And now everyone wants to expel her just for being a divorcee. I'm afraid Celia's just now discovering what men are like. She should put him on a longer leash before he breaks loose entirely."

"You don't really think that, do you, Jordan? Let him be with someone else?"

"Probably not what it sounds like, no. Just make him think he could if he wanted to. Men like the illusion they can still play the game. But deep down, my philosophy is that the further my cowboy strays off the ranch the bigger the alimony check."

"You can't mean that," laughed Christine.

"Well, I'm only half-serious. But you know we can watch something so carefully, stare without blinking, until we begin to see things that aren't really there. Like double vision."

"I guess that's true, Jordan. I never thought of it quite like that. But I still worry about Celia and Steve. She seems so fragile."

"Maybe you should," Jordan added cryptically.

"What?"

"Worry — but nothing to discuss over the phone. You know how the operators like to listen in. And then they gossip."

"Oh, Jordan, sometimes you're so dreadfully cynical. I don't know when to believe you. I think you like mysteries."

"Well, it's better than doing dishes and vacuuming any day, isn't it?! Anyway, I have to hang up now."

"And I suppose that Teddy will wonder where I am, too. Goodbye then," said Christine, hanging up and looking far more troubled than when she had initiated the call.

Chapter 4

Early Saturday morning, the atmosphere drooped over Potawatomi Acres like a heavy moist cloak. Sunrise in the east quickly disappeared, and the horizon to the west darkened, first into a cobalt blue that turned gray and then black. Lightning began to sizzle and crackle — with thunder rumbling in the distance at first, until the explosions of sound almost caught up with the flashes of light as the storm approached. Then, almost as quickly as it began, the rain stopped, and the sky turned bright and warm. The four golfers, who had planned a match to begin at 10 o'clock, had been resigned to hours of waiting and then sloshing through pools of water on the damp fairways and greens, which would hold up their putts like a thick shag rug. The sun parted the damp air to a curtain of steam that hung on only at the edges of the woods, and the course dried quickly.

As usual, the quartet paired into teams. Today it would be odds vs. evens — matching the players from the two sides of the street, hence even and odd house numbers. Dan Clements and Steve Watson would play against Jim Reilly and Teddy Barr. Fortunately, their handicaps were, when added together, relatively equal, and the small bets placed on the outcome accumulated almost no gain for either side, whatever the arrangement. In any case, the competition was almost solely individual, and the teams meant little in the long run. Golf was, as Teddy always maintained, a contest played with and against oneself. It was practically the only sport in which any distraction, be it a tense week at the office or indigestion, could disrupt a smooth swing and the proper address to the ball. This necessity for complete concentration and simultaneous relaxation meant that any of the other players, with a gesture or comment, could prompt a slice or hook into the heavy woods or tenacious rough. But because the four were so accustomed to their Saturday morning matches and one another's quirks, such distractions had, by unconscious mutual agreement, become rare.

Normally, Edgar carried his father's bag, but this morning Marie had insisted that the boy remain at home to clean a gutter that had, in the brief storm, spurted and splashed over the side of the house. Although he hated odd jobs around the house and would miss the dollar earned on the course, he was not unhappy about his task, for he could finish it quickly and then have the rest of the day off. And he wouldn't have to listen to his father's complaints and excuses for his bad play that always embarrassed him.

So the foursome picked up four boys from the caddie master and set out on the brilliant warm, sunlit course, the boys trailing behind carrying their heavy bags. The course itself was laid out in two large conjoined squares, with the clubhouse, parking lot and entrance at the intersection of each half. Although the land was originally flat prairie, the designers had trucked in mountains of soil to build hills and had widened the creek into a hazard that ran through three of the most difficult holes. The holes themselves traced the edges of the square, with the return of the fifth hole beginning at the entrance of Golf View Court. Jim always walked with pride when he passed by the backyard of No. 310, hoping that Jordan would be out in the back scouting the foursome. He had never seen her there and wondered whether she secretly resented his Saturday outings, or perhaps, he worried, she just wished to give the impression of disinterest in something that he prized.

After the game — with the caddies paid off and their leather golf gloves, moist with sweat, packed away, balls washed and separated (for another game or practice) — the four friends walked slowly up the terrace, their cleated saddle shoes crunching on the flagstones. Dan and Steve headed straight to the locker room to shower, but Teddy and Jim lingered. There were about 20 green cast-iron tables on the terrace, scattered around like lily pads on a stone pond. Several were occupied by lounging golfers fresh from the links. A few of the wives had already joined them. As each foursome came up the steps toward the locker room or to sit for a moment in the dying sunlight, they were greeted by friends shouting out scores. Most of the conversations began with dramatic recounting of a hole played well or unfortunately, but whichever way, golfers had learned to describe their results with all the drama of a grand adventure.

Teddy glanced around at the occupied tables as if searching for someone familiar and then reluctantly looked toward the men's locker room. But then he paused, as if changing his mind.

"Looking for someone?" asked Jim, amused to think that his friend must (also) be searching for the long tanned legs and white shorts of Mrs. Smith.

"No, not really. Just seeing who's here and looking for a good spot for a drink. I think I'll sit down here and wait for you guys to change. Unless you want to join me. I'll order something. What are you having, Jim?"

Teddy walked toward an empty table and pulled out a heavy green metal chair, which scraped on the rough surface, and then sat down. Jim joined him.

"I think I'll sit with you for a few minutes," Jim said, still standing. "I can always shower at home; prefer it, in fact. And I wouldn't mind a whiskey sour."

He also pulled out a chair and settled in just as a white-coated waiter approached their table.

"What can I get you two gentlemen?" he asked in a very heavily accented voice.

"Two whiskey sours," replied Teddy without looking up. The waiter backed away from the table and disappeared into a doorway that led to the club restaurant and its attached bar.

"I think that the new Puerto Rican bunch we hired is working out pretty well. Don't you? They seem competent enough. Rotten English sometimes, but what do you expect? You get what you pay for, and they came cheap," said Jim off-handedly.

"Not really sure yet; can't tell," remarked Teddy. "But I like the idea of a single team — one contract, one boss to go to if there's trouble and all one color. Look sharp in those white uniforms, don't they? I mean, some of the women! Nice tight uniforms, brown skin."

"So you noticed, too," laughed Jim. "I've been wondering about them."

"Well, don't wonder too much. At least I don't. Christine can be pretty jealous. And she would know in an instant if I got too interested. She's got some sort of sixth sense about such things. Or maybe our wives have a posse of spies."

"Probably the latter," Jim exclaimed. "They seem to know everything we think, even before the idea occurs to us, like they have some special antenna that catches the broadcast of any impulse before it even becomes an idea."

"Well, maybe so," said Teddy, suddenly turning serious. He looked out over the course, which had turned a darker shade of green in the slanting sun of the late afternoon.

"Where's my damned drink?" he said, suddenly breaking off his gaze and looking around toward the clubhouse.

"Something bothering you, Teddy?"

"You mean besides the slow service?"

"Yep, just wondered."

"Well, if you want to know, I'm just plain bored. Sorry to turn serious on you. I don't mean my job, although that's never been very interesting, just sitting around and making deals and listening to people yelp when we tell them they should have read the fine print in a policy that doesn't cover lost dogs or misplaced jewelry. Yeah, business is OK, I guess, although sometimes I think I've gone about as far as I can. But that's not it."

"Then what?"

"I don't know really. I guess it's home. I'm aging — and the wife is aging. You know, the years seem more and more like a routine and not real time passing by. I think I expected better. And then, the other day, just out of the blue, as if it had suddenly occurred to her — this profound thought — Christine says to me, 'I'm looking forward to growing old with you, Teddy.' And I really had to hold myself back. I could barely speak for a minute. It really caught me with my shorts down! You know how really evil thoughts race into your mind sometimes and stand around, pushing away anything agreeable until you can't say a word because you're afraid of what will come out? Well, that was me! I'm not sure what I'm saying here except that the future looks awfully boring. To grow old together — can you imagine? And more of the same, except worse! What a thought!"

Just at that moment, the waiter returned with two whiskey glasses and set them down with slow precision on the metal table. In the center, between them, he placed a small basket of soda crackers. As he was backing away, Jim caught his sleeve.

"Where's the cherry? A whiskey sour's got to have a cherry!"

"Sorry, sir. We don't got none right now. I could get you lemon. You want lemon?"

Teddy glared at the waiter and then relaxed and took a sip of his drink.

"I'll take that lemon," he said between clinched teeth. "A bit too sweet as it is. And hurry up, before the sun sets," he added sarcastically. The waiter bowed slightly and scurried off.

"I guess it's just not my day," he continued. "Started out well enough, until I dubbed one on the fifth hole. Just couldn't recover after that. My leg began to bother me. The whole round was off; I was off. Happens more and more these days."

"Well, we didn't lose by much," Jim replied. "And Steve and Dan were pretty bad themselves. But tell me, unless you think I'm prying, are you serious about your marriage? It sounds like trouble. I don't mean anything like a divorce; who would want to get skinned for alimony these days? I see it so many times in the quick sales I have to make. Women come out so far ahead financially I'm sometimes convinced they do it on purpose — cash gushing everywhere like an oil bonanza, so much they don't even know how to spend it."

"No, nothing as serious as that, I guess, although mind you, I've thought about it. Who hasn't? No, I'm just bored, and I think Christine is, too, if she'd be honest."

"Ever thought of trying something on the side? Nothing serious, but maybe one of the girls here. I've certainly had ideas."

"Sure. Who hasn't? But in this town, it would be up on a banner in 10 minutes, right under the clock in the town square by the train station. There'd be so much chin-wagging you could hear everyone's teeth chattering. I would never risk it. And then, who could I sell insurance to? This town of small-minded gossips? You know yourself how much we have to depend on trust and respect. This may be a community, community this and community that — until one of us strays! And then!"

There was a long pause as both men turned back to their drinks. Jim looked away as if he were making a decision and then peered at his friend again.

"Well, I wasn't going to mention it," he began with some hesitation, "but do you ever read Esquire magazine?"

"Once in a while, I buy a copy if I'm out of town on business. Pictures and cartoons and all. Yeah. But I don't think much of the clothes. Can't see myself in all that matching stuff and jewelry and chains. And cologne! Who wears that stuff? Nobody here in the Midwest. It must be some pansy in New York who's pushing that."

"I didn't mean the clothes," Jim said, suddenly becoming serious.

He broke off at that moment as the waiter appeared with several slim wedges of lemon set on a small dish.

"Thanks," remarked Jim, looking up. And then he added: "Put it on my tab. Reilly, spelled R-E-I-L-L-Y."

"Yes, sir," said the waiter, disappearing again quickly.

As both men squeezed a few drops of lemon into their drinks, Jim resumed:

"No, I'm talking about an article I read. It really gave me pause. In fact, I was a bit shocked at first, and then I thought, 'I see; I get it.' It had a really tricky title — something like 'How to Spice Up Your Marriage.' I'm not sure why I even bothered to start reading, but, well, I did. Maybe I was just thinking along those lines unconsciously. Anyway, it described a special kind of party. I had never heard of it before and can't say I can quite imagine it even now." He paused, knowing that he had completely captured Teddy's attention.

"It's only played among friends — close friends and couples — not with strangers, and you'll see why when I tell you."

Teddy put his drink down and looked at Jim.

"You certainly are taking your time getting to the point," he said. "Is this like the sales pitch you deliver, all the extras in the house first — the new gas furnace, the storm windows, the latest GE kitchen and the two-car garage — before, wham, you finally lay on the price?"

"Sorry," exclaimed Jim. "It's just such a bizarre idea, and of course, I'm sure you won't be interested."

"How can I be if I don't know what it is?"

"A key party," Jim said in a low, almost conspiratorial voice, as if the other occupants of the terrace had suddenly stopped talking and his voice would carry to every other table.

"A key party?" said Teddy curiously. "Never heard of it."

"Keep your voice down, Teddy, and I'll tell you. It's a pretty scandalous idea. I don't even know why I mentioned it in the first place."

"Now you've got my curiosity up. You just can't leave me hanging like that. Come on."

"OK, I'll tell you if you promise not to be shocked or to laugh. I don't know which would be worse."

"No promises. Wouldn't buy a house from you without an inspection, either, you know, even though you are a friend."

"All right then," said Jim, suddenly relishing the fact that he had completely captured Teddy's interest and that he was now practically begging to know.

"It's a game played among couples who are friends."

"Yes, you said that already."

"The article said it was best to begin with cocktails and a minimum of four pairs."

"Remind me never to ask you to explain something complicated," Teddy broke in. "There's not enough time in the day. How do you ever sell a house?"

"Oh, it's easy. Selling a house is like a courtship. You've got to draw it out slow. Clients expect to be courted and flattered. It's the attention that gets them. Because if you make a sudden move, you'll break the mood and, to coin a phrase, end up with blue balls."

"Ha!" exclaimed Teddy. "But what's this mysterious game, seriously?"

"Well, four couples get together, and after a few drinks to loosen things up, the women take out their house keys and drop them in a hat."

"What kind of hat?" interrupted Teddy.

"Now who is it that doesn't know how to tell a story — or listen to one? Any kind of hat — like the one Steve wears to go to his office downtown. And then, if I may continue, each guy picks a key — not looking, of course — and that's the woman he sleeps with that night."

"Goddamn! And the women would agree, just like that? I don't believe it."

"Yeah, just among friends, and no one ever talks about it."

"Sure," said Teddy, "and women don't ever gossip or compare notes. When were you born, Jim, yesterday?"

"I was pretty sure you wouldn't take it seriously. And I wasn't actually proposing that *we* do it. Just telling you what I read and imagining a bit. And thinking out loud about your problem of boredom."

"Well," said Teddy, a look of puzzlement on his face, "let me take you seriously for a minute. A couple of questions: Can you exchange keys with someone once you've chosen — you know, to trade up, so to speak? And what are the odds of the thing? For example, what are the chances that you'll end up with your own wife or that everyone chooses their own house key? Wouldn't that be a disappointment!"

"I did read the rules, and they answered one of your questions, at least: No exchanges. I think you can see why. That would raise all kinds of problems — bruised egos, jealousy and, worst of all, the impression of taking it seriously. After all, it's only a game, and there always have to be winners and losers. And as for the odds, I don't know. I guess we could figure it out. Probably 1 in 4 that you'd end up in your own bed. And maybe 1 in 16 that all of us would. Those are pretty slim, in either case."

"So you've actually thought about this, haven't you, Jim? I mean, coming up with the odds so quick. But I don't think you're necessarily right about the 1 in 16. Seems wrong to me, what little math I know."

"Well, I've got an accountant in my office who could tell me right off. He's always talking about betting and plays the horses sometimes. If anyone knows, he will. He's a whiz. I could ask him — hypothetically, of course."

"And hypothetically you're just thinking you might like to try this little experiment?"

Just then, Steve and Dan emerged from the locker room door and, spotting their friends, made their way over to the table.

"What kept you two? And I see you've already got a head start on cocktails," exclaimed Steve.

"Such as they are, yeah," said Teddy. "I'm not sure this new crew is up to it. Got myself a whiskey sour made with lemon juice and no cherry."

"Well, give 'em a chance," said Steve. "You know, the board spent a lot of time hiring new staff, and this group came with some high recommendations."

He and Dan pulled out chairs and sat down. As they did, the same waiter approached.

"Can I get you somethin'?" he asked.

"Gin and tonic for me," Dan replied.

"Same," added Steve, "lots of ice." As the waiter walked back into the clubhouse, he continued: "And now you'll have to tell us what this conspiracy is all about. A real estate deal? Some secret new golf swing? Something to change the odds in your favor?"

"Well, yes," laughed Jim, turning slightly red. "We were discussing odds. But not about a golf game."

Chapter 5

Late in the afternoon, after a few more rounds of unsatisfactory drinks, Jim Reilly stumbled home, stepped around the dog, who seemed to be lurking at the front door, and called to Jordan:

"I'm home," he shouted.

He waited a moment, and then, hearing no answer, he hung up his light jacket and trudged loudly up the stairs, knowing that his wife did not like surprises.

"Where are you?" he called again. He heard muffled sounds from the bathroom adjacent to the bedroom. He walked over to the door and said gently:

"I'm home, Jordan."

"Yes, I heard you the first time," came the reply.

He hesitated to try the door because he suspected it would be locked. He had often wondered about this cloistered habit of his wife's — whether she feared an intruder or just wished to shut him out until she had applied her usual thick barrier of makeup, lacquered her hair and put on whatever foundation garments she used to pull her body into shape. It had been a very long time, he mused, since he had seen her naked, and the memory of her body had become almost entirely tactile now — as if he were a blind man groping her torso, as opposed to a lover in the light. He put his fingers on the doorknob gently and gave it a slight twist.

"It's locked," she cried out. "Use the bathroom downstairs."

Jim retreated and sat down on the bed. He was not looking forward to the evening's cocktail party at the Vollmers' at the end of the street. It was scheduled to begin at 7, which meant no dinner and only the slim cocktail sandwiches that Sarah Vollmer concocted out of deviled ham and cucumber and dark bread or some kind of pungent fish paste that turned the taste of a cocktail into something like the flavor of bitter medicine. He knew that with two drinks already in him, he was already teetering on the edge of a severe drunk that evening, and the Vollmers would be of no help at all, pouring drinks and topping off glasses until he lost count. He often wondered whether this ritual was some sort of erotic plan, because as the evening wore on, Sarah would become all hands, touching her male guests lightly and swinging her lithe body from one corner of the living room to the other, glancing around to see who was watching. She seemed busier and busier as the night wore on — and her movements more and more like a seductive dance. John Vollmer paid no attention to these sexy ministrations and usually chatted amiably with Jordan or Celia or the other women as if he were one of their kind. Jim wondered about him sometimes because it didn't seem natural that a man — a real man — should show such ease at the center of a group of chattering women. He knew he could never hold court in such a fashion. What would he talk about? And, he anticipated further, when he got home that evening, he would already have a piercing hangover to compete with his hunger pangs. He would face assault, as it were, from both ends of his body. And there were houses to show on Sunday — and no leisure and no golf and probably some angry words from Jordan, her way of maintaining a safe distance from any advance he might chance.

It angered him that his imagination worked in this way, compounding and scheduling unhappiness like filling in the spaces of the day's calendar. He wondered whether he wasn't just as much a party to his unhappiness as Jordan. Maybe he was just making excuses and blaming her.

~~~

Steve and Celia were also dressing for the party. Steve had decided to wear a dark blue suit that evening. There was sure to be a chill by the time the gathering started, and he always liked to be overdressed on such occasions as if to emphasize his position at the bank. Celia, on the other hand, could not make up her mind, and she paced the bedroom in her white slip and nylons, trying on one outfit after another. Each time she slipped on a dress, she turned to model it for Steve, who sat on the bed.

"How about this one?" she said, zipping up the side seam of a pastel green sheath.

"OK," he said, glancing briefly at her. "Fine."

"But I mean really! 'OK' isn't much encouragement."

"Very pretty," he corrected himself.

"You don't mean that at all, and you're not even looking at me," she replied. And she quickly unzipped the dress and threw it angrily on the bed.

"Maybe the pink," she said, pulling a dress off the hanger in her closet and stepping into it. It was a tight-fitting silk-satin dress with puffy sleeves gathered above the elbow.

"What do you think?"

"That one's OK, too," he said absently.

"You're not helping," she said, her voice rising almost to a shout. "What are you thinking about? Some other woman? I watch you, you know."

"Yes," said Steve, glaring at her. "I know you watch me. Just wear anything you like. It's not a command performance, you know. And anyway, why do you care what I think? You only get dressed up for the other women, not me. And I've watched you, too, all of you, crowding around each other, paying compliments to each other about some dress you've worn a thousand times or some new hairstyle that makes you look like a kewpie doll. Do you really mean all that billing and cooing?"

"Don't be cruel," she said. "That's really cruel. So I'll wear the green, since you seem to prefer that."

Steve stood up and shook his head in disbelief. He walked out of the room and downstairs. Entering the empty family room, he stood for a moment, looking around as if assessing the placement of the furnishings. Then he strode over and sat down in his favorite chair and looked out the picture window onto the darkened lawn and the careful flower beds that edged it. Now that the leaves were beginning to fall, punching out spaces in the wall of green and yellow at the very end of the garden, he could dimly make out the roadway behind and the lights of one of the houses that bordered it. He had certainly driven on that other street behind his, many times, and he knew the names of some of its residents. It was the job of a banker to know everything he could about the families of a town, and he knew superficial facts about bank accounts and loans. But he had no friends among them, and he wondered about their lives. Maybe someday he would drive over and look carefully at their houses, assess whether or not it might be rewarding to find a friend or two there. It was, he sometimes felt, limiting to be such close friends with the others on his street.

~~~

Marie Clements sat waiting anxiously for Dan to call her. If there was anything she hated, it was to be late to a party. Leave it to Christine and Teddy Barr to make a grand entrance when the party was already in full swing. Christine's excuse always sounded as if the event was a distraction from other, more important obligations. And Marie thought that Teddy would be easy to handle, pliable and punctual. No, it was intentional on Christine's part, a purposeful disruption, the midact entrance of the long-awaited (aging) diva sweeping into the room and catching everyone's admiring eye. But what, really, was there to admire? Christine had always seemed to Marie to be a stock figure from an advertisement for a washing machine or a new car, a cartoonish character, never attractive enough to draw attention away from the product, only reassuring the consumer that it belonged in the average home — very average.

"That's mean-minded," Marie said to herself, "but if she just wouldn't put on airs!"

Marie continued to muse. Why was she herself always so late? Well, she had her boys to contend with — a meal, warnings repeated several times about driving around with friends and getting into trouble. Marie didn't even want to think about what her two teenage sons might have planned for that evening. She only knew that their relationship was a series of dares and challenges that no number of dire threats could unsettle. And Dan was useless when it came to the boys. He either was too soft on them, citing his own misbehavior as a youth (but who cared in that small southern Illinois town with few cars and the constraints of Prohibition?), or barked like a hanging judge, delivering sentences that she knew she was expected to carry out.

"Are you ready, Dan?" she called out finally.

"Sure. Have been for half an hour. Just let me get my jacket. I'll meet you outside in a second."

"Goodbye, boys," she called out, not quite knowing where they were. "And remember what I said."

"Yes, Mom," came a single disembodied voice from upstairs.

Unconvinced that her words, if repeated once more, would have any added effect on the selective hearing of her sons, she picked up her white Angora sweater with the rhinestone swirls, shrugged it over her shoulders and stepped out to the driveway. Dan was already in the driver's seat of the Buick and had the motor purring softly as a kitten. They drove the few short blocks to the end of the street. They might have walked, for it was the briefest of distances. Dan had once calculated, based on the length of the parallel fifth and sixth holes together, that the street was no more than 1,000 yards long. But there were no sidewalks on Golf View Court, so walking was difficult. Indeed, according to Jim Reilly, that omission was one of the surest signs of an exclusive neighborhood. He even recounted once, laughingly, that a whole section of their town had petitioned to have the sidewalks removed so that their lawns could be extended down to the street. Only the expense and the precedent had prevented the town manager from moving ahead, and besides, there had been a small and vocal coterie of opponents who questioned the sanity and the motivations of the anti-sidewalk contingent. Marie was happy to keep things just as they were — and enjoy the envy of others. Common folk, she thought.

By the time Dan had parked the Buick in the Vollmers' driveway behind the Reillys' Pontiac — he loved to hem in other cars so that a couple might have to ask him to move if they intended to leave early — the party was well underway. Finding the door ajar, the Clementses walked in, Dan pushing ahead of Marie, abandoning her in the hall.

The living room they entered was glowing with warm light that came from soft spotlights buried in the exposed wood beams of the ceiling and from floor lamps, which cast their light back upward, merging the two illuminations in the middle. The only really dark edge of the room was the glass wall, through which it was possible to see the close-by indistinct shapes of trees and bushes outlined by the reflection cast by the indoor light. A slight wind made these shapes move slightly, like slow-motion dancers in shrouded costumes. The floor, paved in a dark red tile, showed only at the edges of the room, for an enormous Turkish rug filled the center. All the furniture was modern and casual — two squarish matching sofas set on straight wooden legs and upholstered in a burnt orange fabric and several low tables, one of them strewn with magazines, including The New Yorker and The Atlantic. One wall was entirely covered by a bookshelf and a record player. The lowest shelves bore a matching leather-bound set of the "great books." John Vollmer had explained at an earlier party that there were 52 volumes in all, chosen by a committee of the most distinguished professors from the University of Chicago and containing all the knowledge of the world — or at least that which was deemed necessary for the contemplative life. Steve Watson had once jested, when the foursome of friends had passed by the Vollmers' at the seventh tee, that he had opened the first volume of the set once and that he could swear, from the crack of the binding and the thin layer of dust on the cover, that he was the first ever to do so.

On one wall hung several large abstract paintings, chosen, it would appear, primarily to complement the orange, brown and amber color scheme of the room. The only really personal items visible were several small photographs set in metal frames resting in the middle of the bookshelf and showing Sarah and John in various poses during their recent European trip. The fourth wall was a large limestone fireplace with polished brass andirons holding two logs. The interior was charred with black creosote deposited by the numerous fires that the Vollmers burned in winter months.

After Christine and Teddy Barr had finally made their expected late entrance, Sarah Vollmer, with a dramatic sweep of her arms, gathered in their attention. She had positioned herself in a pool of light that fell from one of the overhead lights in the center of the living room.

"Please, everyone," she began, clapping her hands, "just a minute so that I may introduce you to my distinguished friends from the University of Chicago."

Her voice then fell to a tone that seemed to Steve, who was listening carefully, to be the pitch of reverence.

"They've come all the way from downtown: Mr. and Mrs. Mark Spiegel — actually Mark Spiegel and Candice Overmann. They write under their bachelor names. Perhaps you've heard of their wonderful book on child rearing, "Modern Character and How to Shape It." You really must read it if you haven't. It's so intelligent and thoughtful — all the most modern theories woven together with such skill and practical advice."

Dan turned to Marie and said very quietly under the slight murmur of the other guests: "Probably lots of Freudian hogwash. Leave it to the Vollmers to dig up friends like that."

Marie turned to look at Dan and smiled. "I can tell a University of Chicago face anywhere," she said conspiratorially. "Look at her hair, parted right down the middle of her head like a man. And that short gray hair, cut like a cocker spaniel! It's so aggressive to make yourself intentionally plain with no makeup and... What is it she's wearing, a Polish peasant dress of some sort?"

"I guess you mean she looks Jewish, don't you?" Dan whispered softly.

Sarah spoke again: "Please introduce yourselves, everyone. I'm sure you'll all be fascinated."

She stepped aside and, as if in an afterthought, added, "And please serve yourselves drinks, or better yet, ask John to make something special for you."

Several of the men headed to the dining room entrance, where the Vollmers had set up an elaborate assortment of glasses and bottles, in what looked from a distance like a miniature glass cityscape, a skyline of scotch, bourbon, gin, sherry, low tumblers, wineglasses and a large bucket of ice.

The two special guests stood somewhat forlorn next to the cold fireplace until Sarah walked over to them and handed each a drink. Spying Celia standing alone, she rushed over, seized her by the arm and steered her toward the couple.

"This is Celia Watson," she said. "Steve, her other half, is no doubt standing at the drinks table. Yes. There he is," she said, pointing. "But, Mark, you really must tell Celia about your new project. And I'm just dying to know more about it myself."

Celia held out a limp hand to Mark and said "hello" in the miniature voice that she often used in greeting strangers. She just nodded to Candice.

"Very pleased to meet you, Mrs. Watson. Are you one of the group that Sarah has been telling us about, of friends who all live along this beautiful street?"

"Yes, I suppose we are."

"Then you're very fortunate. It's lovely out here. So many trees and lovely yards. So different from Hyde Park."

Sarah interrupted. "But, Mark, you really must talk about the new book. What's it to be called?"

"'Beyond Companionate Marriage,'" said Candice, who suddenly wedged into the conversation. "You see, we've done an enormous amount of research among couples of various ages and their habits, and now we've written up our conclusions — our surprising conclusions, I should add."

"But I don't understand 'companionate marriage,'" replied Celia meekly. "Of course, I know the words, but what do they mean?"

"That's simply marvelous!" exclaimed Mark. "It's just the curious reaction we had hoped for. Companionate is an old theory. The idea was that men and women should be more or less equal in a relationship — therefore companionate, like friends and companions. That was certainly a fine idea — good for its time, at least — and we applaud it, don't we, Overmann?"

He paused to allow Celia to realize that he had called his wife by her last name, thus granting her fellow authority.

"So we still do, more or less, endorse a form of equality in marriage," he continued, "but that hasn't gotten us very far, you see, and the whole theory has led to a great deal of unhappiness and dashed expectations. We think that — unfortunately — divorce would be significantly more common in the United States if it were easier and not such a permanent blemish and burden on the divorcees."

"So this is a book that proposes simple divorce?" said Celia cautiously.

"Oh, no, not at all," broke in Candice. "What we suggest is to understand and take seriously the different needs of the two sexes and how they can be expressed in ways that complement each other. In other words, a complementary marriage. Men and women just aren't the same, as I'm sure you know. And we believe you can have a wonderful and fulfilling relationship and still be partners if — and only if — you take these differences into account. After all, there are many levels and types of partnerships." She stopped for a minute and looked carefully at Celia:

"Do you have children, Mrs. Watson?"

"Please — Celia. No." She looked distressed at her admission. "But I really have always wanted a daughter, but Steve doesn't—"

"That makes it absolutely necessary to compensate, then, doesn't it?" interrupted Candice. "You see, if two partners want or think something different, then there has to be negotiation and compromise. And it's important not to forget biology. Yes, the trick is to balance biology and psychology."

Celia looked around and spied Steve standing next to Jordan Reilly, two drinks in his hand. She looked at him intently for a moment, pleading for rescue, but he was talking rapidly, perhaps telling Jordan some sort of story and paying no attention to her.

"But do you have children, Candice?" she asked, hoping to pry open the jaws of some sort of trap she felt had snapped shut on her.

"Oh, no," said Mark, answering for his wife. "You see, we've decided to be professionals, both of us, and—"

Sarah interrupted. "Tell Celia about your findings on fidelity."

"Oh, yes, indeed," replied Mark. "Well, it may surprise you that 'infidelity' — not the best term for it, I think, because it's so negative — infidelity, for want of a better word, is often helpful in a marriage to overcome boredom. Because boredom is the greatest hindrance to happiness. At least that's what our informants tell us."

"So you're advocating adultery. Hear! Hear!" broke in Jim Reilly, who had sidled up to the conversation long enough to hear Mark's last sentence. "That will certainly sell a lot of books! Don't you want a drink, Celia? Looking at your face, I think you need one. Where are Steve's manners?"

He held out his glass and offered it to her. "I haven't touched it yet."

"Thanks, Jim," exclaimed Celia, gratefully seizing the drink. She looked around anxiously. "Oh, there's Steve. Very nice to meet you." She flung a brief wave at the two writers as she turned to escape. But Jim remained, his curiosity piqued. He studied the two researchers for a minute, saying nothing. He wondered how it was possible to connect the man with the shiny bald head and droopy jowls and his intensely plain wife — who, he noticed, wore no makeup — with sex and passion. Perhaps, he thought, this was the meaning of "objective research"; you had to erase anything interesting about the way you looked or what you believed for the sake of science.

"You're smiling, Jim," commented Sarah. "Something we were saying?"

"Oh, no," Jim mumbled. "I just wanted to introduce myself to your guests. Jim Reilly."

He held out his hand, and Candice Overmann seized it and gave it an emphatic squeeze. Her husband's grip, however, felt limp and warm like the paw of a dog extending its leg to beg.

"The Spiegels were talking about their new book on couples," said Sarah, putting her arm around Jim's waist to urge him closer into the circle of four. "It's most interesting what they have discovered. But you should tell him, Mark."

"Well, as I was saying, we feel that most advice books about marriage — although ours is certainly not that — have been caught up in an older idea, trying to make men and women the same. I suppose that's the effect of the war and all those women working in factories. But of course, wartime is unnatural, and the mix-up of sex roles was expedient and temporary. Millions of men ripped from their families, never seeing a woman — at least not someone accessible emotionally. And the women heading up families and even working as machinists."

Candice broke in: "It was a terribly distorted time, and then, when it ended, we just swung back to the other extreme. If you don't mind my saying so, you live in the midst of it. I don't mean you personally, Jim, of course, but 'you' meaning 'the suburbanite.' I assume that none of the wives out here works, except for dear Sarah. And there is such confusion about proper sex roles nowadays. You see, we have to find a way for men and women to be happy in a relationship that isn't absolutely equal or fundamentally unequal — something that allows the different psychologies of men and women to develop in a harmonious way, if I can use a musical analogy. Men and women are born and mature in a different way. Marriage must thus be a resolution of that dissonance."

Jim looked puzzled for a minute.

"I can see that you don't understand," said Mark, his pale skin flushing. "Let me put it simply: Men and women develop differently; they have different instincts, almost two human natures. That worked well enough in primitive societies, where life was short and nasty and brutish. But now the contest is not against nature and to survive but to be happy. So life's principal struggle is emotional and psychological. And speaking frankly of the basic human trait that is both physical and mental, we have gone from a world where sex was entirely practical and necessary to the survival and progress of civilization to where reproduction is only incidental, if at all — where having children is fulfilling instead of compulsory. You know that the opposite of the word 'fulfilled' is 'frustrated,' and that is a key concept in our work. So in a way, it's come to a reversal of human nature. The desire to reproduce is now just a tiny fraction of existence, yet the contemporary marriage equation is not about pleasure or completion or satisfaction. Children remain the focus, and not the relationship. So all of the dark and mysterious and buried human instincts have to be refocused before they turn destructive. I think you can see where I'm heading, can't you? To be completely frank, men don't need to change or repress their instincts so much. They are actually the more malleable and modern half of the species. It's women who do. And they suffer for it. Let me be simple: Unfortunately, women now control the sex act because of its association with childbirth, and that results in all sorts of distortions and burdens. Just saying 'yes' or 'no' creates mammoth problems for both partners."

Jim looked incredulously at Mark and then Candice, and it flashed through his mind that Jordan certainly fit their description, with her repertoire of refusals and the small hints that led to bigger and then obvious ones if he ignored them, until the thunder came.

"And if men allow women to control sex, to give to them the right to say 'no' on a whim, that can become a habit and lead to all sorts of psychological disorders. To put it most plainly: For men, sex is yes, and for women, it's maybe. And you can't have such insecurity in a relationship; it isn't healthy." With that pronouncement, Mark tittered and then became quiet, searching Jim's face for agreement and understanding.

Sarah laughed nervously. "Well, that does sound interesting. And now," she said in a louder voice, "everyone, how about another drink? Why don't you get something, Jim, while I introduce the Spiegels around? We don't want to monopolize them."

Jim thought for a second that this abrupt intervention might somehow be a comment on what the two psychologists were saying, but then he remembered how frequently Sarah was brusque and even thoughtless, as if she only half-listened to what others were saying. It was part of what defined her eccentricity. But he was, he realized, taken by the arguments of the Spiegels and thought that he might look up one of their books at the library, because he had no intention of bringing it home. And for the second time that day, he thought of the 'key party' idea and his discussion with Teddy.

As the evening passed into night, groups shifted, as if standing in one combination after another was a slow dance accompanied by the gurgle and splash of drinks being poured and the soft clunk of ice cubes being dropped into empty glasses. The canapé trays now contained only crumbs. Most of the women had stopped drinking or slowed to an occasional sip, but several of the men, Dan Clements most noticeably, were on their fourth round. Marie had tried, just once, to slow him down, but he waved her away brusquely.

"I'll know when I've had enough, Marie," he said, grabbing back the glass that she had slipped out of his reluctant fist. "Just stop watching me. Why don't you go and talk to those professors? They're your sort — cultured! And they look sober to me!"

"Keep your voice down," she said in an urgent whisper.

"Why? What's the matter? Are you afraid you'll learn something new about sex? It wouldn't hurt, you know," and he laughed at his joke.

"That's hardly funny, Dan. You'll regret this in the morning. It'll hurt your golf game to play with a hangover."

"I'm more concerned with the regret I'll encounter when we're back home — my punishment. What'll it be tonight, the silent treatment or just the headache? And aren't I the one who's supposed to be having the headache?"

Marie glared at him with eyes that narrowed in anger and hurt. Dan thought, for a moment, that he saw the flick of her pink tongue. But she turned without a further word and sought out Celia and Christine, who were chatting with John Vollmer.

"Yeah," Dan called after her, leering and unsteady. "Join the ladies!"

Marie swung around angrily; her mouth dropped open as if to say something, and then, deciding against it, she walked on determinedly.

When the evening ended, at 11 or so, it was as if all the guests at once decided to leave. Teddy Barr grabbed Christine and whispered to her: "I'm ravenous. Let's go home before I faint with hunger."

Christine laughed but decided he was right. The evening was definitely over. "Wonderful time," she chirped to Sarah. "And as usual, such fascinating guests. Are they going back to Chicago tonight?"

"So glad you and Teddy could come. No, we'll put them up in the guest suite tonight."

Seeing the move initiated by the Barrs, the other couples drifted toward the front door, where Sarah and John positioned themselves like an earnest footman and butler. When the guests had all emerged onto the front driveway, the front door closed. Only the bright twin spotlights that came from the top of the garage pushed the dark night back, reflecting on the shimmering metal of the parked cars.

Marie guided Dan's uncertain path to the Buick and opened the door, swinging it all the way out. She shoved him roughly into the passenger seat, closed the door and walked around to her side.

"I'll drive," she said once she had adjusted the seat forward and started the motor."

"Sure," said Dan. "Sure."

~~~

When the Watsons got home, Celia immediately climbed upstairs after hanging up her coat in the hallway closet. Steve went into the kitchen and stood for several minutes looking into the open refrigerator. Finally, he picked out a half-empty bottle of milk and drank some of it, until the taste curdled in his mouth. By the time he reached the bedroom, after carefully brushing his teeth, he saw that the room was entirely cloaked in darkness. He sat down on the edge of his wife's bed, leaned over and nuzzled her wispy blond hair with his mouth. She stirred, and he put his hands under the covers, feeling the silky nightgown that clung to her thighs. She turned abruptly and mumbled: "Just hold me tonight, Steve. I'm cold and afraid."

"Of what?" he asked, surprised."

"Something vague. I don't know. Don't ask me. Just hold me for a minute."

Chapter 6

When the golfing foursome met on the first tee on Saturday morning, the weather had turned gray and blustery again, whipping the towel of the ball washer and bending high branches of the trees to look as if they were shifting a heavy burden.

"Don't like this kind of weather at all," said Teddy Barr, shading his eyes. "It makes my leg hurt," he continued, explaining in advance why he might play badly, "and it'll probably rain before we get through the first nine. But I'm game to start anyway. Get the fog out of my brain."

"Good idea," laughed Dan Clements. "Had a couple too many last night. Strange people, weren't they, those two birds from Chicago? Leave it to the Vollmers."

"But it was kind of interesting, what I heard of it," broke in Steve Watson, "even if it was utter nonsense. But I think we live in an era of nonsense," he added pensively.

"I actually thought it made a lot of sense," remarked Dan. "I talked to them both for quite a while. They're strange-looking ducks, I'll grant you, but what they had to say about a man's need for leeway in a marriage and not to feel tied down and in bondage to women — all that rang a bell, at least my bell!"

"Well, look who's the professor now," replied Teddy. And then, changing the subject abruptly, he continued: "I think it's me and you today, Steve, against the up-road duo — across-the-street teams this time."

"Yeah, it's the fifth-hole neighbors vs. the seventh-holers. Only I doubt we'll even get that far before the weather sours even more. Damned Midwest winter coming on! I think we'll take a vacation to Arizona this year so I can do some winter golfing."

"Nice idea," said Dan without looking at Steve, "especially since you've got bankers' hours."

"OK, guys," interrupted Jim Reilly. "We'd better get started, and that means our side tees up first, so, if you will, Dan.

Dan walked over to his bag, held upright by his caddie, and extracted his driver. As he bent over to tee up his ball, he remarked, "A good day for a hook with this wind blowing, at least on the first three holes!"

He carefully put on his leather glove and snapped it and then took two practice swings, one of which caught a small divot that hung in the air for a moment until the breeze flung it aside. Concentrating on his shot, he rocked his body to dig in his cleated soles and then swung the club loosely over the ball two times. Finally, he rested the head of the driver on the ground next to the tee, hesitated and then jerked his arms backward in a broken arch, the club falling slightly at the apex, his wrists cocked. When he swung down on the ball, it exploded with a click, sped quickly in a rising parabola — shifting slightly from left to right — and landed with two bounds in the fairway.

"Well, you've done it, partner," cried Jim. "No permanent damage from last night — at least that we can see. You're up next, Steve."

~~~

The foursome made their way through the first five holes, playing evenly and playing badly. Dan's first shot was his last that went true, and he splayed his woods and irons across the rough and into traps and once lost his ball under a pile of leaves in the fringe of woods on the fourth hole. His bad luck seemed to infect the others, partly because they were now rushing their shots and conceding to one another longish, difficult and dubious putts. Soon the rumble of thunder swept down the empty corridors of the fairway, and lightning crackled across the western sky, momentarily lightening the scene in an eerie, almost extradimensional greenish light.

I think we'd better head for shelter, and quick," said Teddy. "We're going to get drenched. The caddies can wait it out in the shelter near the fifth tee. And if you want, we can probably make it to my house or, better, Jim's."

"That's fine with me," Jim said quickly. "Let's make a dash for it. We can sit in the den until the storm passes. Something this intense and sudden won't last long."

The caddies raced for the small shelter and then ranged the golf bags along the back wall to keep them dry, while the four players walked quickly, single file, on a path through a border of trees and into the back garden of the Reilly house. They made it to the overhang on the veranda just as the rain began to pelt down, slapping the leaves that had fallen on the ground like hail. The wind blew the rain up against the picture window of the den in gusts, and Jim Reilly quickly swung open the unlocked door. They could hear a high-pitched barking from somewhere inside.

"Just wait here, gentlemen," he ordered. "I have to get the damned dog out of the way; he'll bite everyone otherwise. But come in and sit down. I'll be right back."

He walked across the room, up two steps of the landing and out through the door. The barking stopped suddenly, and then the men could hear him calling: "Jordan, Jordan, are you home?"

After a few minutes, while the bedraggled players stood waiting, Jim reappeared, carrying an aluminum ice bucket. He closed the door and stepped into the room.

"No one home but us trespassers," he joked. "Dog is in the kitchen and out of trouble. Sit down, everyone. I assume it's not too early for a drink."

Without waiting for an answer, he walked over to a large cabinet with glass doors and pulled out three bottles — gin, bourbon and scotch — setting them on the wood/Formica top.

"The three venal sins," he quipped. "And if you want something less deadly, I've got beer in the fridge. But I thought you would all want a shot of something stronger until the storm passes."

Just then, a blast of wind and rain rattled the window, and it seemed for a moment that the air in the room had become electric.

"It may be a while," said Teddy Barr, motioning to the gloomy scene in the back garden, with its twisting trees. The galloping wind had already trampled a bed of cornflowers and daisies and scattered leaves and small branches everywhere across the lawn.

"Yes, it won't be long before winter," said Jim, doling out drinks.

"Scotch, Teddy, if I'm right? And bourbons for you and Steve, Dan?"

"I really hate winter," said Dan. "I mean besides not being able to play golf. I can never get used to downtown when it snows. You guys are lucky working out here close to home. It's unbelievable some days when the wind comes howling off Lake Michigan. Colder than a witch's--"

"Speaking of which," broke in Steve, laughing. "I'm reminded again of that odd couple last night. Especially her! What a demon! What a pair!"

"I don't know; didn't talk to them that much," interjected Teddy. "But one thing I understood was that they were some sort of sex therapists."

"And didn't they just fit that job title," said Steve, "gray, dull and plain. Must be what drives people to study sex rather than enjoy it! I think there must be a word for people like that."

"Hear! Hear!" exclaimed Teddy, looking rather despondently at his drink.

"But," said Jim, "you have to admit that some of the things they said made sense — about how women always control sex. I'd never thought much about it, but I guess I'd have to say — in my limited experience, of course — that it sounds accurate enough. And I can agree; it certainly is a problem."

"Hey, Jim," interrupted Teddy, gulping his drink, "if you're starting down that road, I'll need a refresher."

"Sure," he replied, and he stood up to seize the glass that Teddy held out to him. He swished around the half-melted ice cubes. Same?"

"Yeah, if you don't mind."

Jim walked over to the table and seized the bourbon bottle by the neck and poured a generous amount into the glass. With a set of stainless steel tongs, he dropped two ice cubes into the glass and then turned around.

"You'd better all drink up," he said. "I have something serious to ask you." He gestured with the glass to include them all. "It's something not exactly serious, but, well — Teddy already knows."

"You don't mean," Teddy blurted out. "I was sure that you were kidding the other day. Come off it!"

"Well, I certainly was, at first, until I thought about it. And then considering what that pair was suggesting last night. So now, I'm actually thinking about doing it."

"So what's the great mystery?" interrupted Dan. "Or is this a secret plot you two have been hatching?"

As he spoke, there was a flash of lightning, followed by an almost immediate crash of thunder that shook the room.

"Well, now you have my attention," Dan laughed, "if you can call on the gods for punctuation!"

"Not quite as dramatic as that," continued Jim. "I have a suggestion, I mean a proposition."

"That's sure the right word for it," said Teddy, sipping his second drink. "I think I may need a third shot to listen to this — or maybe some more ice." He stood and walked to the drinks cabinet and plunked a new cube of ice in his glass and splashed a finger of bourbon over it.

"OK, OK," said Jim. "Anyway, I told Teddy about it, and now I'll fill you two in. You see, there was this article in Esquire magazine that I read..."

"Jordan lets you bring that in the house? I'm really impressed," said Steve. "I'd never hear the end of it from Celia. She would question me about every risqué picture or cartoon and then quiz me at the end of every sentence if I still loved her."

"So you've read it, too, then, Steve," interjected Dan. "Otherwise, you wouldn't know what's in it."

"Sure. Who hasn't in the barbershop? While you guys have your noses buried in Superman and Wonder Woman comics, I admit, I've glanced at it. It's actually got some fine literature in it — short stories and reviews — and, I don't mind telling you, some really useful hints about what they're wearing in New York."

"Surprised you didn't see this article, then, since you're a regular reader," Jim continued, winking. "But let me finish, I mean start."

"Go ahead, then," said Teddy. "I can see you're determined. We won't interrupt again."

"The article was called 'How to Spice Up Your Marriage.' It described something called a key game and then itemized the rules. Apparently, it was based on actual events in suburban New York — Long Island somewhere or maybe Westport. I don't remember. Anyway, it takes four or five couples, all close friends around the same age, that you can trust. It's pretty simple, really. All the girls put a spare key to their front door in a hat. Then the men, without looking, of course, just pick one out, and that's who they spend the night with."

There was a moment's silence, and then Dan gave an embarrassed laugh: "That's just pure fiction, designed to sell magazines. I'll bet it never happened. Just some copywriter's imagination. And no one would ever agree to that, especially not our wives."

"You might be surprised," replied Jim. "They get just as tired of the same old two-minute drill as we do. Might put some life back into the routine."

"God," cried Steve. "I can just see Celia's face if I said yes! I'd be locked out forever — instead of just the usual wildcat strike."

"And how do you know what house belongs to which key?" asked Teddy. "I mean, if you did it, how would you know where to go?"

"Each key would have a number taped to it and a master list with the numbers opposite the address. And there's one important rule. Everyone has to swear to secrecy; no one can know — ever — who sleeps with whom. Breaking that rule, and the magazine put this in bold type, could wreck the playfulness of the game and turn it into real adultery — with all sorts of complications and jealousies. Not to speak of what the community would say."

"Damn it, Jim," said Teddy in a loud voice. "What the hell? Are you seriously suggesting that we play this game?"

"Maybe," said Jim.

"Celia would never agree. It's as simple as that. I know her too well," exclaimed Steve.

"And anyway," broke in Dan, "let's talk about odds for a minute. If you had only four couples, aren't the odds pretty high that you'd end up with your own wife? Wouldn't that be even worse? You agree to adultery and end up with the usual bitter tears and rejection. And besides, that isn't what swinging — isn't that what they call it, swinging? — is all about. Five couples would up the odds considerably. Maybe the Vollmers could be persuaded. That Sarah is pretty hot, always slinking around, suggesting—"

Teddy laughed. "So you know that word swinging, huh, Dan? Not so naive as you put on. And as for Sarah, there's John to contend with, and I don't think he goes in for women much that way. One of our wives would be awfully disappointed."

"Or relieved," said Steve. "But tell me, what about the odds? I mean, isn't it one in four that you'd get your own wife? That would be the 'unluck' of the draw, I guess. And the odds of everyone getting their own wife, one in 16?"

"Not so," interrupted Jim. "Yes, one in four is right for one of us, but something larger than that for all of us: 24-1."

"How do you figure that one?"

"My accountant is a genius with numbers," said Jim, "because I'm not and someone has to be when you're in the real estate business. So I just asked him to figure it out."

"You mean you told him to figure out the odds for a key party?" interjected Teddy. "You've got balls!"

"Of course not. I just made it an abstract math problem — four people, each with a different-colored chip. Made it sound like some sort of poker game, although I know he prefers to play the horses. Anyway, that's what he told me. So it really would make the game almost pure chance."

The four men sat in silence for a moment. And then, suddenly, the dog began a frenzied yapping and whining. A door slammed in a distant part of the house, and they heard Jordan calling out: "Jim, are you there?"

"Down here, honey," shouted Jim.

The door opened with a bang, and Jordan stood with her hands on her hips, looking at the disheveled and embarrassed foursome.

"This place smells like a distillery," she said with a disapproving frown. "Why in the world?"

"The storm," said Teddy, gesturing with his drink, "the storm. We just ran for it and left the caddies and our bags in the shelter."

"We'd better get back then," said Jim. "Hardly noticed, but it isn't raining anymore."

"Nice to see you, Jordan," said Dan politely, getting up. The others followed him, with Jim pushing ahead to lead the way out of the back door and into the garden. As they slogged along the path back onto the course, every motion of the wind brought a brief shower of rain down on them. But when they approached the shelter, the sun flashed momentarily through the clouds, and a mist rose from the edges of the woods. The caddies trudged out to greet them, hefting their heavy bags.

"Can't remember who's up exactly," said Dan, "but why don't you tee off, Teddy?"

For the rest of the match, the four players struggled with wet grass and putts that halted suddenly on the soggy greens or went askew along a rivulet of matted grass. On occasion, they had to suspend the rules when a ball dug into the soft ground. But surprisingly, there was among them an air of jollity, perhaps because it was so difficult to be competitive in the miserable conditions and there was always a ready excuse for a bad shot. When they finally reached the 18th green, the sun was shining in a blue, crystalline sky, washed clean of any trace of clouds. An insistent breeze began to blow from the north as the cold front passed through. No one had spoken further of the conversation in Jim's den, and no one suggested sitting on the veranda on the wet iron chairs for a drink.

~~~

That evening, after dinner — during which Jordan seemed peeved and abrupt, her movements jerky and robotic as if some force were compelling her to place the plates on the table and then stack them afterward with a clumsy clatter — Jim finally asked what was bothering her. The answer was swift and not entirely unexpected:

"You and your golf buddies messing about in our den."

"My den, you forget, Jordan," he shot back immediately. "It's my den. And so what if we have a drink in the middle of the day? I don't worry about your bridge parties and what goes on there — all that gossip and girl talk."

"And what gossip do you think you are talking about?" she said with a surprised look.

"Well, nothing in particular. Look, let's not argue. I just happen to believe that when you get together with your friends, after you've exhausted the compliments you pay each other about makeup, hairstyles and some new outfit, then I think you really dig in and exchange secrets, about us..."

"I don't talk about you," she replied harshly. "And there isn't really much to say that would interest anyone anyway."

Jim just glowered at her and then stood up. "I'll be in my den (he underscored the words) if you want me," he blurted out. "And then early to bed. I've got to show several houses tomorrow."

Jordan also stood, and without a word, she picked up a stack of dishes and headed into the kitchen. As she did so, she was greeted at the door by Sammy, wagging his tail energetically and jumping up on his hind legs in anticipation of some choice table scraps. But Jordan seized him by the collar and pushed him out of the kitchen. As she closed the door behind him, she mumbled, "Go bother your father."

~~~

Across the street, when the Clements family finished dinner, Dan and the two boys went outside to play basketball by the floodlights installed over the garage doors. As they approached the driveway, Dan handed two sets of car keys to his younger son.

"Park the cars on the street, OK?" he asked. "And don't gun the Buick. Your mother will have a fit!"

"You mean you'll have a fit, don't you, Dad?" Dan Jr. replied with a chuckle. He then began his assignment of moving the two cars to make space for the game, fully enjoying this bit of sanctioned lawbreaking and proud that his father had already taught him to drive, practicing up and down Golf View Court.

As he did, Edgar began to dribble the ball and then lofted a shot over the raised hands of his father. The ball drifted up out of the arc of light and into the black canopy of night and then fell back and into the net with a whoosh.

"Good shot, son!" cried Dan. "I can see you've been working on it."

"Right-o, daddy-o. I can take you any day," he exclaimed, catching the rebound and dribbling past his father. Just as he was about to shoot, his younger brother stepped into the ring of light and blocked his path. The ball skittered away, and Dan picked it up and threw up a shot that rattled around before it fell off to the side.

"Sons against dads," cried Dan Jr.

"For sure," exclaimed Edgar. "What's the point of playing unless it's a real game — man against man, teens vs. the aged? You taught me that!"

"That's a bit unfair, isn't it? I'm only one dad. But OK," he agreed, thinking proudly for a minute that this was the best part of his marriage — two healthy sons and a great house and a lot of horsepower.

~~~

Of the four men who had golfed that afternoon, only Steve was troubled that evening by the conversation during the storm. During a dinner where he found himself staring at Celia's pale, bland face, so much so that she furrowed her brow into the quizzical look that she had used many times before to question his silence, he finally said — without waiting for her to ask — "Nothing. Nothing at all."

"I didn't say anything," she shot back in her mouse's voice.

"But I know that look," he replied. "And it's nothing. I was just thinking." As he said that, he instantly regretted his words.

"About what?"

"Nothing," he repeated.

"But it must be something. You seem so far away."

"Nothing. It's just that I played so badly today. After the storm, it was impossible. The course was a swamp."

"Well, don't blame me," said Celia, reassured that this was perhaps the reason for his sullen mood.

But Steve wasn't thinking about golf at all; rather, he was thinking about her, in a way, and wondering whether Jim Reilly was really serious and whether Teddy had already agreed. He found himself imagining the possibility of sleeping with Jordan or Marie, even Christine, and he felt a faint stir as he did.

"No," he said to himself. "No, it would never happen, if for no other reason than Celia would refuse vehemently. She was too logical and timid and jealous. (Which among all her petty hesitations and fears would dissuade her, or would they all?) Something such as this would destroy their marriage, even to suggest it. Yet he had to admit to himself that he was bored; he felt cramped and caged, like one of the tellers at his bank, sitting behind a metal screen all day and handing out money to fund someone else's pleasure.

"Steve," said Celia loudly. "Where are you? Are you having some sort of argument with yourself?"

Steve blinked self-consciously and turned away, as if she were able to read his thoughts in the image of his eye. Was this what marriage meant? "The marriage of true minds" — he remembered that line from the sonnet that his brother had read at their wedding ceremony. Was theirs a marriage of true minds, the erasure of individuality and their merger into something so common and conjoined that each knew the other's thoughts and anticipated words not yet spoken? Somehow this idea disgusted him.

Chapter 7

That Monday when evening was beginning to close around Golf View Court and the streetlights atop the concrete pillars flickered on — intensifying the impression of dark beyond the reach of their glowing peripheries — Steve Watson turned slowly into the street. As he approached the Clementses' house on the left, he could make out Dan reparking his big Buick in the driveway. He tapped his horn lightly and pulled up to the curb and stopped. He rolled down his window. As Dan emerged from his car and slammed the door, Steve shouted at him, "Hey, Dan! Just getting home?"

Dan turned and walked slowly to his friend's car.

"No, just putting the car away for the night. The boys were using the driveway to work on their bikes."

He leaned into Steve's open window, resting his arms on the doorframe.

"What's up?"

"Oh, nothing. Just saying hello. I was out running an errand for Celia and saw you. I thought I'd stop."

"Glad you did. Say, are we still on for golf this Saturday? At the regular time?"

"Wouldn't miss it. Hope the weather will hold. I don't relish another storm like last week."

"Well, I'll see you then," said Dan, straightening up and tapping the car frame gently as if he were patting the flanks of a horse to spur it to ride off. Steve didn't move, however.

"There is one thing. I just wanted to ask you without Jim and Teddy around. Did you think about what they were talking about? Were they really serious?"

"You mean that game of chance — wife swapping — that Jim suggested? Yes, I actually do think he was serious; at least he thought he was."

"So, what do you think? I mean, I can't imagine it."

Dan paused and stole a look back at his house.

"I can think of a lot of reasons not to risk it."

"Is it just the risk that worries you?" replied Steve abruptly. "I mean, isn't there a lot wrong with it? If bad consequences were the only reasons not to act, I'd say you'd be able to write a debauched novel about every man, woman and child in this town — lust and crime combined."

"From what I understand — and of course it's only what Marie tells me, or rather, hints at — there's a lot that happens in this town that you and I don't ever hear about. Like a pressure cooker, this place heats up fast. Those were her very words."

"So then you're not afraid to do it — if there are no consequences, that is?" asked Steve.

"There are always consequences." Dan laughed. "And anyway, I can predict it isn't going to happen. It was just a lot of big talk and Jim wanting to sound sophisticated and worldly. I'd say that half the trouble in this town comes from too much ambition and the other from putting on airs. The things my kids tell me about their friends: always bragging about something. I don't know how the so-called community would act if a scandal really broke out into the open."

Steve chuckled to himself as he looked past Dan, at the sleek convertible parked in the driveway.

Dan caught his eye and said: "OK, I suppose you're right. Point taken. But Marie insisted on having it. And it's actually a great car and a great buy."

"Yes, of course it was," agreed Steve. "Well, I'll be off now. See you on Saturday."

He turned the key of his Chevrolet and pulled away from the curb and into the street.

~~~

When the four friends met for golf and drinks the next Saturday, all their talk was about the game and the busy chatter of men who knew one another too well to indulge in any serious talk. Like the members of a family, they repeated the same comments and half-finished sentences and familiar gestures. This was a small company of men who had hidden their emotions beneath the banality of the expected; they were entirely comfortable in their superficial companionship, not wanting to dig into the treacherous terrain of emotions. Yet beneath this light banter and evasive talk about hooks and slices and putts and the state of the economy, Jim, at least, felt a growing tension. Usually, he ascribed this impression to competitiveness. No one of the group really wished to admit it, but Jim thought, or at least he suspected that he knew by ascribing his own thoughts to the others, that this was, in some respects, a cutthroat competition. No matter how they paired, each player had a double nemesis. There was the struggle each man had against himself, fighting his handicap — what a telling word! — to come in lower than the accumulated history of all his scores. And then there was the struggle against the opposing pair — in addition to each man's desire to play better than his partner, hoping to surpass him in leading to victory. This was, Jim thought, the way of true brothers.

But today, he felt, there was something else in the air. Dan and Steve, teamed together, seemed to be passing messages between them, as if they had developed a special language of looks and had come to some sort of decision. Jim thought he knew, of course. They were upset, maybe even appalled, by his suggestion of a key party. Or maybe, he thought, these were guilty looks passed between them because, despite anything they may have said to each other, they were intrigued. What was the lawyer's phrase that Dan sometimes used — plausible deniability?

After the game ended and the caddies were paid off, the four men sat on the veranda, watching the dying sun. And then, as if from nowhere else but some internal conversation with himself, Steve stood up from the table and said, "Before I leave, I'm instructed by Celia," he began, "to remind you about next Friday night at our place — our anniversary party. And she insisted: No presents, just your presence."

"Wouldn't miss it, Steve old boy. My condolences!" said Teddy. "How many years of the ball and chain now?"

"Twenty."

"My God!" exclaimed Dan. "Is it that long? No wonder."

"No wonder what?"

"That hangdog look — all droopy ears and floppy jowls. No wonder you shot 95 today," said Teddy, laughing.

"Hey, look," replied Steve with feigned anger. "You've been hitched even longer than I have. And speaking of old dogs..."

"That can't learn new tricks if they tried," interjected Jim. "Yes, we'll all be there soon enough. Wouldn't want to let you go through this by yourself, Steve. What are friends for, after all, except to attend the wake?"

"Ha-ha," said Steve sarcastically. "Sometimes I'm not sure," he continued, "but at least your friends will be around to remind you of time passing by too quickly. 'I knew you when you were just a pup!' Isn't that the line?"

"We'll be there," said Jim. "To mix a metaphor: because we're all in the same boat as you."

"Or hitched to the same harness," added Teddy.

When the others had gone to their separate cars, Steve wandered back from the parking lot to the terrace and sat down. He wanted to shake off his bad mood before he drove home and decided not to leave yet. An acquaintance two tables over shouted at him to join their group, but Steve just nodded and raised his hand to signal 'no, thanks.' When the waiter appeared, he ordered a beer, because he was already feeling fuzzy and wanted something light. The cold, he thought, would restore him for the drive to Golf View. He watched, without interest or focus, the players on the 18th green. They were just blurred images in his mind, visionary figures whose actuality did not register, and if someone had asked him to identify them — and he knew most of the club members at least by sight — he would have had to look again. When his drink came, he wrapped his hands around the cold bottle and stared at the empty, waiting glass the waiter had set in front of him.

He knew this feeling well, this sense of disassociation — when he could step outside himself to look through the emptiness of the moment, when his senses were dulled and everything around him was a blur — and only a vague feeling of uneasiness registered. He thought to indulge himself in this place of abstraction, but the cold sensation of the beer bottle in his grip brought him back to something he did not wish to think about: the anniversary party. He had always dreaded such events, not because he wanted to be free of Celia — not that at all — but for the same reason that he hated New Year's Eve parties, with their forced gaiety when in fact they were just the commemoration of the loss of a year and of aging, missed opportunities and boredom. Anniversary parties also simplified and smoothed out and flattened all the complicated feelings he had — and that he knew Celia shared — about their marriage. All those maudlin and sentimental toasts — the forced jokes, the strained smiles and the compliments — allegedly to help celebrate the accumulating milestones along an imaginary straight road. In fact, however, the path of any marriage — and his especially — was filled with torturous switchbacks and dangerous precipices of emotions. Anniversaries falsified a marriage because they only commemorated its survival, its longevity. That was it, he thought. Nothing could be said of the reality of conflicts and joys and the flurries of anger and regret. He knew he would have to get very drunk.

~~~

The Friday morning of the party, Sarah and John Vollmer sat together sipping coffee on high stools along the gleaming wooden sideboard that ran the length of their kitchen. Perched there, they could look out of the casement windows that gave onto the garden and beyond, to the patch of woods that almost encircled their house. They wore matching silk robes, in white with rainbow pockets and sashes. This was a favorite time of day for both, although it usually passed in silence, with only an occasional stray noise from outside breaking their passive reverie. But today Sarah was animated, and she made small fussy noises that her husband recognized were a cue for him to inquire.

"You seem rather restless today, dear," he began. "Is something the matter?"

Sarah smiled at the understanding between them, the result of years of intimacy, which had created an action-reaction partnership between them, wherein the smallest motion was part of a catalog of shared, if almost unconscious, signals that substituted for the question or comments that would initiate a discussion. But this flicker of pleasure passed quickly as she revealed the motive of her uneasiness.

"It's the anniversary party of Steve and Celia tonight. It's not that I don't want to go. I've always liked them, and it's nice to celebrate such an event. And it's nothing that Celia has actually said. But I just have the feeling that there might be something happening between them. And those four couples — such an intense lot of friendships. Is it healthy, I wonder, to be so exclusive? And that makes me feel sometimes as if we're the spare tire, ready for a roll in an emergency but not part of the vehicle." She laughed suddenly at her choice of metaphors. "And wouldn't you know it, that dish we're supposed to bring is a dessert. That's like an afterthought and not part of the main course. And I can guarantee that someone will refuse it for being on a diet."

"Well, I hope you're not feeling insulted," said John, reaching over to pat her hand.

"Of course not — well, not really. It's just an observation. I just like to be sure of where I stand."

"So you don't care that much."

"Only out of curiosity. My participant-observer research of the suburbs."

"Ah," replied John, laughing, "the Margaret Mead of Golf View Court."

"Mm-hmm," she said. "In a way, yes, I imagine that's so, but they are our friends, too." She paused and turned to look at him. "You don't think that I look like Margaret Mead, do you, John? What a horrible thought! All those years of living with Indian tribes. Why, every line and wrinkle is like the documentation of another dry season. She has a face like a wilderness map drawn on rawhide. I hope you don't think of me that way."

"Of course not."

But Sarah had already moved on from looks to intelligence and was not yet satisfied to let the comparison go:

"On the other hand, she is brilliant, and I think she understands the sexes better than almost anyone."

"There you go. You see?" said John, trying to recover his innocence from the insinuations of his initial remark.

"But you have solved one problem for me," Sarah continued. "I know what I'll wear tonight: all silver and turquoise and dark blue, a symbolism that means something just to you and me."

"Just no buckskin or feathers!"

"No," she laughed, "And now, if I can just think of a dessert that's appropriate for 20 years of marriage."

"How about that tinned plum pudding someone gave us last Christmas? Don't we still have it somewhere? That surely carries a certain remembrance of time vanished."

"You really are wicked, John! And I suppose you'd suggest hard sauce, too. I'm not sure the message is exactly appropriate. No, I think something light, airy. I suppose a chocolate angel food cake. Yes, that's it."

"I take it that there's a note of irony there, too."

"However you want to take it, John. And now, get out of my kitchen. I've got work to do."

John scurried out, taking his coffee cup with him, and Sarah walked over to the shelf that held her cookbooks. She selected a thick volume and let the book fall open on the kitchen counter. She thumbed through the pages and then stopped. Walking to the long cabinet next to the sink, she pulled out two large crockery bowls and then glanced at the Mixmaster, which stood at the end of the counter like a silver insect, its mandibles raised up. One after the other, she began putting ingredients out to set beside it — eggs, flour, cream of tartar, vanilla. She looked in several places but realized she was out of chocolate.

"Darn," she muttered, and then she called in the direction of the living room.

"John! I need you for an instant," she called.

"I'm here," he said, almost immediately peering around the doorframe as if he had been stationed at the margin of her workroom waiting for the errand that he supposed would come.

"Be a dear," she said, glancing briefly in his direction. "I need some chocolate, cocoa, the powdered kind. You can't miss it at the store. And you can always ask if you can't find it."

"OK," he said, disappearing. "I'm on my way."

~~~

Celia Watson sat in the living room on the couch that had just acquired new slipcovers in white with an abstract floral design of green and rose. Before her, on the coffee table, she had spread open a photo album and four book-sized wedding portraits framed in tarnished brass, propped up by the cardboard, velveteen wedges on their backsides. Only one of these was normally on view, but she had pulled the others out from the top shelf of her sewing room closet. She looked carefully from one to the next and was so absorbed that she did not notice Steve standing in the doorway that led into the dining room and watching her intently. On more than one occasion he positioned himself this way, half disguised and half in view, curious about what she did alone, how her face moved and her expressions when she thought no one was watching. He had discovered that these small, almost unconscious movements revealed her moods better than anything, and certainly better than asking. And if he ever wondered why he did this, he told himself that after many years of marriage, he still understood her only slightly and never quite knew what to expect — the fury of some hidden anger, the surprising weakness of clinging affection or just ordinary Celia in a good humor. As he watched, she picked up one photo frame after another, stared at it and then replaced it on the table.

"What are you doing with those old photos," he asked finally.

"Oh, it's you," she said, startled and flustered that he had caught her in such a pensive and unguarded moment.

"Yes."

"I'm just looking at our wedding pictures. Comparing smiles, if you must know."

"What on earth?"

"You see, I thought I'd take several of them out for the party tonight, put them around the room for people."

"But why smiles? And what's the difference?"

"We were so happy then."

"And aren't we happy now, Celia?"

"Oh, of course we are. Just not in the same way. Don't you think it was the most wonderful day, our wedding? I sometimes remember it like yesterday."

"Seems to me that it's all old history by now. Every year, those photos look younger and younger. I can hardly remember anymore."

"Don't you remember, Steve? Don't you want to remember? I certainly do. Even your brother's rambling toast. We were so innocent then, laughing at ourselves. The things he said about you. I never imagined that…" Her voice trailed off.

"Really? Imagined what?"

"I don't know exactly. The ordinariness of it all. The routine. The seasons passing. Golf and bridge and golf and bridge. All the games we play. I'm not sure what's even real anymore. Do you think we'll ever grow up and actually do something? Sometimes I think we never should have come here; stayed in Chicago. Things would have been different."

"And so you expected more?"

"Of course I did," she blurted out, picking up one of the pictures and clutching it to her slight chest. "Everyone hopes for more. Didn't you? I guess I just wanted that precious beginning to go on forever and not to spiral down into—"

"That's not realistic, and now who is it that won't grow up?" Steve said, turning to walk out of the room. "You make your own unhappiness and boredom and carry them around with you like the keys in your handbag. You know that, don't you? Or do you? Do you really know what you want?"

"Well, I'm sure I don't want your realism," Celia called to his retreating back. Taking the picture she was holding and putting it facedown on the table, she thought fiercely, "I'm not boring!" She stood abruptly and piled the framed photos on top of the picture albums and carried them up the stairs to her sewing room. Seeing the closet door open, she thrust the pile onto the highest shelf and then, for good measure, gave it another shove until she heard the dull snap of glass cracking. She turned and tried to slam the door, but it only sighed and rebounded as it bumped against a mound of loose bolts of cloth, pillows and suitcases lying on the floor. She turned and walked over to sit down on the tapestry bench in front of the sewing machine and stared at it until the image clouded over.

"I won't cry," she murmured. "I won't," she sobbed quietly.

~~~

Before going upstairs to dress for the party, Christine Barr found Teddy sitting in his favorite easy chair, reading the sports section of the Chicago Tribune.

"Haven't you finished with that yet?" she questioned, leaning into the dim living room. And why don't you turn on the lights? I need to talk to you about something."

"Does it need light?"

"That's not funny, Ted. You're just making a joke. But I have something serious to discuss."

"Yes," he said, rustling the newspaper as he turned the page but still not looking at her.

"Did you read Sandy's letter?"

Setting the paper aside now, Teddy folded it carefully to save his place, as if to signal his impatience. Whenever their daughter was the subject, he knew they would disagree — not with any consistency, however. They had a way of circling around each other's opinions, seizing on a vacant argument that the other had either overlooked or just abandoned. Sometimes, he thought, this was like a dance before a mirror, in which each motion reflected its opposite. They never settled anything, just took on each other's old arguments.

"So what do you think?"

"I don't think it's a good idea," replied Teddy. "She's only a freshman, after all. Going to Europe with a group of students, at her age, what's the point?"

"I thought you would probably say something like that. But it's a splendid opportunity. And there will be a professor to chaperone." She paused. "Surely, you can't object to the cost. I'll pay for it, of course."

Teddy stopped himself from replying for a minute, for he deeply resented his wife's reminder that her money, her family's money, financed almost everything they did that was slightly out of the ordinary.

"No, no," he said. "It's just that Europe is so run-down and old. Didn't we just rescue them from yet another catastrophe? All that death and destruction for nothing! Why doesn't she take a trip to California and look at the future, not dusty old museums and ruins?"

"Because the tour doesn't go to California! And anyway, there are such wonderful sights, such an opportunity to see and absorb culture." Christine stopped and then almost shouted. "Sometimes, Teddy, I think that all you ever think about is golf. Maybe if you had more of a career, you wouldn't be…"

"Be what?" he demanded angrily. "Be what?"

"So tedious." She stopped herself from voicing the alliteration that suddenly popped into her mind. "Tedious Teddy, Tedious Teddy." She turned and stalked out of the room.

~~~

Marie Clements sat at the dressing table, which was set in a wood frame the shape of a painter's palette. It was strewn with bottles of perfume and makeup jars. Surrounding the mirror, facing her, was a fringe of small bulbs, which gave off a stark white light, revealing every line and flaw in her face. She had wanted this harsh light, for no other reason than it revealed everything — all the blemishes and imperfections that she needed to disguise. For she was nothing if not a realist about herself, and she had become as skilled and deliberate as an impressionist painter at creating the idea of beauty on the canvas of her face. The suggestion of mystery, the play of light and dark and reflection were the purpose of her wizardry. With all that and her exquisite and expensive taste in clothes — which always tended toward a tailored look, slightly masculine and thus commanding — she was a master of artifice.

Behind her, sitting on the bed and pulling on his socks, Dan admired her back and the image that reflected on the mirror. Although she was aware of his stare and could feel the warmth of this rapt attention, she did not seek to catch his reflected eye but instead accepted it for what it was: the pride of possession. Marie flushed slightly at the thought, for to be possessed by a man, as she understood it, was to exercise great, if cautious, power over him by being the slightly elusive object of ownership. Of course, Dan was unaware of her manipulations and would never quite understand how his fascination with her as an object gave her great sway over him. She could, if she wanted, provoke jealousy and discomfort, for she knew that in making herself attractive to him, she would invite the looks of other men and the hesitant admiration of women, whose obvious delight and interest only strengthened Dan's sense of precarious ownership.

"Are you about ready?" he said, feigning exasperation.

"Almost," she said. "I have to finish here and then get the dish we're taking to the Watsons'. I know they absolutely forbade any presents, but I couldn't resist buying them a dinner plate I saw at Field's. It's wrapped next to the casserole in the kitchen.

"China? I thought this was the year of paper."

"Don't try to be funny," Marie replied, pursing her lips tautly to apply a careful line of brilliant red.

"Well, I guess china is an appropriate gift for 20 years — something delicate and expensive and, if I know your

thinking, very fragile. Just a whole bundle of symbols —
the cost of the piece in commemoration of the years and
breakable to symbolize the future. I guess when you get
to gold, it's as permanent as death or a bad tooth."

"Or diamonds for 60 years — all sharp edges and
glittery. You're very philosophical tonight," she said, rising
and shutting off the makeup lights. "Hand me that top,
will you, dear, on the chair."

Dan picked up the embroidered jacket and passed it to
her.

"New?" he asked.

"Of course. And now I'm ready." Putting it on, she
stood before him, one foot thrust slightly forward.

"Beautiful as ever," he said admiringly.

~~~

"Martini?" said Steve demandingly as he greeted each
guest at the door. "Special anniversary gin I bought just
for tonight. You only get one variation: an olive — or
maybe two — or not."

Celia watched this ritual with amusement. She knew
that her husband thought to put guests at their ease by
this brusque order, even if it was to press on them a drink
they would prefer not to have. At least he believed that
such a welcome broke the ice, but she knew, after many
years of watching him, that it came from an innate
clumsiness, an inability to relax and just let the warmth of
friendship carry a conversation or meeting. He hated the
eddies of silence that often meant nothing more than an
affirmation of unremarked pleasure, so he charged in,
commanding and controlling, fearing those moments

when the talking lagged. To an outsider, this might have seemed only like an uncontrollable gregariousness. But Celia knew, on the contrary, that it was a device to control — for Steve to control others and her and as a way of covering over the vague waves of self-doubt that a disjointed conversation stirred up in him.

Celia, on the other hand, stood back, almost shy as the guests arrived, for it was her job not to offer drinks and jollity but to accept the dishes for the potluck dinner and arrange them on the dining room table or place them in the oven for warming. Her function was, as she thought about it, to carry out orders. And now, she thought, here she was standing at the door like a hired receptionist at someone else's party.

Sarah Vollmer, when she arrived with the silver-covered cake dish, was, as usual, casual and generous, offering to carry her contribution to wherever Celia wished it placed. But Jordan Reilly was precise and demanding:

"This goes into a warm oven for 10 minutes or so, 350 degrees," she said as she shoved a large casserole dish into Celia's hands, and then she went off into the living room to follow her husband.

Christine, whom Celia counted as her best friend, however, offered to help and took her offering into the kitchen before accepting Steve's martini.

When Marie and Dan finally arrived, unusually late, Steve noticed that Marie was carrying a gaily wrapped package. He put it down without comment and called for Celia to accept the covered dish that Dan carried. After greeting her last guests, Celia backed away and then pushed open the swinging door that led from the kitchen to the dining room. She heard Steve saying in a loud voice, "You have some catching up to do." She guessed he was addressing Marie or Dan. "We're, most of us, on our second round already. Except Celia, of course. Come on in and join the party. You, too, Celia," he said, raising his voice. When she appeared in the living room, he walked over to her with a brimming martini glass.

"I put an extra bit of gin in it for a jump-start!" he laughed.

"Wait," cried Teddy. "Just a minute before everyone has their next drink. Jordan and I brought a bottle of Champagne."

"Why not wait until after dinner?" broke in John Vollmer. "Then we can have a proper toast and a real salute to Celia and Steve."

"Good idea! I want to get sloshed!" agreed Steve. "So let's have that second round now." He walked over to the table, holding a large ice bucket, a jar of stuffed green olives, several gin bottles and an open bottle of dry vermouth. Pouring a whole bottle of chilled gin into a large glass canister, he added a slosh of vermouth and then placed the jar of olives next to the fresh glasses.

"I really just believe in passing the bottle of vermouth over the gin. It's a bit like sprinkling it with a dribble of holy water," he said.

"Nothing if not for the strong-hearted," laughed Sarah.

Steve took a glass stir stick and agitated the mixture, clanging the sides of the glass bowl. Then he splashed about a half-cup in each glass."

"You can choose whether it's olives or not. Personally, I like mine straightforward and honest."

Each of the guests approached, one at a time, for a refill.

"Awfully solemn bunch, aren't we?" remarked Jordan as the group fell silent. "You'd think this was Communion or something."

"Rather like it," laughed Steve. "I do feel like I'm distributing indulgences. Drink up, everyone."

Celia took a sip of her drink and then called to Christine: "Will you give me a hand putting out the food? If I have another one of these, I won't be able to lift a fork, let alone serve."

"Of course," replied Christine, hastening toward the dining room.

The table was already set up with Celia's best dishes — an old bone china set with thick gold rims, which had belonged to her mother. The heavy silver knives and forks and spoons (also from the family treasury) were spread out in three fan shapes for easy retrieval. At the end of the table lay a pile of monogrammed linen napkins, which she and Steve had received as a wedding present. The overhead chandelier made the arrangement sparkle with a dim gleam. Christine and Celia, after heating up Jordan's dish, brought out all the contributions of the guests, setting them in a row that began with an elaborate Waldorf salad and ended with the chocolate angel food cake.

"Just let me get some small dishes and cake forks for the dessert," said Celia, "and we'll be done."

"What a lovely table," exclaimed Sarah, who had wandered into the dining room. She put her arms around Celia's shoulders and hugged her. "And what a lovely occasion."

When the table was completely prepared, Celia stood under the archway between the two rooms and clapped her hands.

"Dinner is ready," she cried over the muffled din of conversations. "I hope you don't mind eating alfresco."

"Oh, God, Celia," said Steve angrily. "You use Italian just because you think it sounds sophisticated, but you always mangle it. That means 'outside'!" He paused briefly. "Stupid mistake," he muttered. "What you really mean," he continued loudly, "is 'eretto, ritto, in piedi' or 'seduto in salotto' — to eat standing up or sitting in the living room. Those are the best translations I can come up with. At least those three miserable years of mine in Italy during the war have some use! Anyway, everyone, you know what she intended to say: Grab a plate, and I hope you won't spill anything on my nice clean carpet."

Celia said nothing but just glared at Steve and then turned her back. Christine put her hand on Celia's arm and bent to whisper to her: "He's just nervous. It isn't every day that a man celebrates his 20th wedding anniversary."

"I just wish he wouldn't drink so much," replied Celia, pushing away. "It makes him so mean."

Despite this flicker of temper, which died out quickly, the partyers enthusiastically moved into the dining room to fill their plates. Celia and Steve, standing in opposite corners of the room, waited until everyone had finished getting food before joining their guests, who were standing (Teddy) or sitting on the sofa with their plates resting on the coffee table or ensconced in chairs with their food balanced on their knees. The difficulty of maneuvering knives and forks and precariously balanced plates dampened the conversation except for an occasional compliment to whoever had brought the chicken casserole and the green beans and almonds and the salad. It was an entirely unsatisfactory way to dine, but everyone treated it as a necessity of the evening — not really taking pleasure in it but enduring it.

When this rushed interlude had ended and the last crumbs of Sarah's cake had been scraped off the china dishes, Celia and Christine began to stack them to carry them into the kitchen. But Jordan, who had made no effort at all to help, intervened.

"Oh, no, you don't!" she cried. "Just leave all that. You can clean up anytime. This is a special moment. Jim, get out the Champagne, and let's have a toast to our old friends here. Would you get the bottle, someone? I put it in the refrigerator, and of course, we'll need glasses. And I think someone brought a present that you ought to open."

Christine, thinking this order was directed at her, scurried into the kitchen, followed by Celia.

"You know, I don't have any Champagne glasses. I hope wine glasses will do. I think I have enough. We'll have to make do," Celia said. "And could you look for the present on the hall table? I think Marie brought it."

"Of course. I'm sure it's fine, and don't worry. Sometimes Champagne can be an imposition if you don't know it's coming — more trouble than it's worth. Sometimes Jordan — well, she just doesn't always think things through."

Celia found eight glasses and arranged them on an embossed tin tray and followed Christine out of the kitchen carrying the frosty Champagne magnum.

"Hey, don't shake it like that!" cried Jim, grabbing the bottle. "Here, let me open it."

He took a handkerchief from his pocket and, after unwinding the wires that were twisted around the neck, slowly turned the cork until it popped out.

"Not a drop wasted," he cried, "if I may say so myself. And now, everyone..."

When each guest had a glass, he rapidly turned around the room and poured out a small portion into each, the bubbles and froth scenting the air of the room with alcohol.

"Since I'm supposed to make the toast, I will. But in two parts — first briefly, so that the Champagne won't flatten out into ordinary white wine, and then some other words of salute. Anyway, Celia and Steve, our best wishes to both of you, the first of our best friends to reach the 20-year mark. Congratulations!" He motioned his glass at them and then drank with the rest of the group.

"And now a bit more about the history of you two. It seems to me, if I'm not wrong, that not only are you the oldest and longest-married of our friends but almost the first pioneers on Golf View Court. I can remember very well when Jordan and I were looking at houses — thanks to Reilly Realty, if I can give myself a little plug here. We drove down the street, all the way to the Vollmers' turn-around (actually, that house hadn't been built yet), and then drove back. I'm sure we had met because of the bank, and so we stopped off to see you, Steve. It was great to anticipate friends so close, and then Teddy and Christine and Dan and Marie moved in almost as soon as we did. By the way, you engaged a different estate agent, Dan, and I'm not sure I'll ever forgive you for that. But Steve very quickly introduced everyone around, and he was certainly right to suggest that we would become good friends, as some of us on the street would become a quartet of golfers and bridge players. What he said about you, Sarah and John, when we saw the sort of house you were building — well, he predicted you would never play golf or bridge. But you seem to have overcome that failing." He laughed. "And here we are, all close friends anyway."

"And when we moved in," said Marie, "I remember that there was a parade of neighbors who called, one more curious about us than the other. I had the sense of auditioning for some part in a play."

"No," said Jordan, "we just wanted a fourth for bridge!"

"Anyway," continued Jim, waving away any other interruptions, "it's been great to have you as the stalwarts of our special little community here, and we celebrate you both on this most serious of occasions."

"Yes, yes!" they all exclaimed, draining their glasses.

"And now," said Jim, who was obviously pleased to be in command, "I have a question for you two before we start on some serious drinking. Why not tell us how you met?"

Celia and Steve looked at each other, each waiting for the other to begin. Finally, Steve said: "Why don't you tell them?"

"All right," she said meekly. "But only if you promise not to interrupt."

"Only if you don't get it right."

"I think we need another round of drinks," exclaimed Teddy, making for the table to refill his highball glass. "You, Christine? Marie? I think I'm switching back to something harder. Champagne is good enough for toasts, but that fizz isn't for the serious drinker."

"To begin with," said Celia hesitantly when he had returned, nervous about commanding an audience, "it was March 26, 1936. I remember that date because it was exactly a week before Mother and Father were due back from their Florida vacation. I had returned early out of sheer boredom with sand and beaches, and I had the North Side town house all to myself."

"I see a plot thickening already," said Dan. "Girl left on her own, bored out of her wits, unchaperoned, like ripe fruit in an untended orchard."

"Shut up, Dan!" cried Marie. "It's her story, not yours!"

"Anyway," Celia began again, "I was by myself — aside, of course, from the cook, so not entirely unchaperoned as you so gracefully put it, Dan. I was having tea in the living room. Something caught my attention. You know, we had a big bay window with a love seat built into it. It was actually an alcove of glass looking out onto the sidewalk and the street and one of my favorite places to sit."

"Love seat," murmured Dan as he took a healthy swig of his drink.

"Yes, it was. And that afternoon, I heard a commotion outside — someone shouting, and I'm afraid what he was saying wasn't very nice."

"That will have been Steve, no doubt, introducing himself," interrupted Jim. "I can just imagine the scene."

"Guilty," said Steve, raising his glass and spilling a portion of it down the side and onto his sleeve.

"So I looked out," said Celia, plowing on and trying to ignore the disruptions to her story that seemed to make it more and more difficult to tell and almost vulgar. "I looked out and saw this man dressed in a white shirt, sleeves rolled up and light-colored trousers struggling to open the front hood of his car. So I just watched and waited until it became almost comic, like a silent movie — you know, with those exaggerated antics and wild facial expressions like Harpo Marx. I couldn't really hear everything he was saying, but he was obviously very angry and frustrated."

"Sounds like a perfect prelude to romance and marriage," interjected Teddy caustically. He thought he could see that Steve disliked the comparison.

"Finally," Celia plowed on, "he managed to raise the hood and then almost disappeared into the motor. I think I looked away for a while, maybe to pour some tea, but then turned back when I heard a shout. I turned again, and there he was, standing straight again and covered from head to foot in grimy oil, a furious black imp, cursing the automobile. Well, I really felt sorry for him. He looked like a nice man under his blackface, and so I called Della to go out and take him a wet towel. When she appeared, he looked back at the house, at the bay window where I sat, and he waved at me."

"Is the punch line coming soon?" asked Teddy, who was obviously bored by Celia's long dramatization.

"I'm sorry. I'm coming to that right now," she replied. "And after Della returned, she came into the living room and announced: 'He wants to wash off with a garden hose or something, miss. But it would mean him tramping through the house.'"

"'No,' I said. 'Tell him to come around through the alley, and I'll unlock the back gate.' And so Della went back out and directed him down the block. I went through to the kitchen to wait for him, and that's how we met."

"A great story and very romantic," exclaimed Jordan.

"But she's forgotten half of it — or censored it, anyway!" cried Steve. "The important half."

"Steve, don't," said Celia sternly. "Just don't you dare!"

"But why not? We're all adults here. No one is going to judge you."

"Does that include you?" she shot back.

"But you forgot to tell the end," Steve chided her. "I rinsed some of the oil off, but my clothes were ruined, so you invited me inside. I guess we had a long chat first, but I pretty much knew what would happen."

"Steve, please!"

"I came in, and you let me wash off in the bathroom upstairs. And then you gave me some of your dad's old clothes. I must have looked like a scarecrow, because everything was too big and I just flapped every time I moved. You were kind enough to give me dinner, and then you sent the cook home. It was quite a night, and we ended up in bed — your parents' bed, I think."

"Damn you, Steve!" shouted Celia. "What will they think of me?"

"I think it's wonderful and romantic," said Sarah. "Don't be ashamed, Celia."

"But you'll all think I was desperate or something — an easy touch."

"A lot easier than you are now," said Steve in a voice that was scarcely audible.

"Damn you again, Steve! How dare you?!"

"I need another drink," said Jordan. "I think we all need a refresher."

She walked over and poured two fingers of scotch (because the martini canister was empty) into a glass and then clunked an ice cube in.

"Anyone else?"

There was a pause until Christine exclaimed: "I forgot Marie's present. Here," she said to Celia, "open it."

Celia took the package from Christine's outstretched hand and quickly ripped off the wrapping paper. It was a Wedgwood plate, a sky-blue color with a raised white border around the edge and the figures of a man and a woman embracing in the center.

"Oh, it's lovely," cried Celia. "Look, Steve!"

She started to hand it to him but released it before he had a firm grip, and it fell to the floor, grazing a chair leg and splitting in two.

"Oh, dear," exclaimed Marie, jumping up from her seat. "And look. It's split in pieces, and the two figures are separated by a jagged edge. I'm so sorry. I'll buy you another one — tomorrow."

"Don't bother," said Steve. "It's not important. You meant well, and I guess I'm just clumsy tonight. Or Celia is. Doesn't matter."

Celia said nothing and just sat down abruptly. Steve walked toward the dining room and called back, "I think I'll have another drink then. Anyone join me?"

"Not for us, I fear," said Sarah, rising out of her seat. "I think John and I will be going. I have a dance class to teach tomorrow morning. But it's been such a lovely party, Celia, and a wonderful occasion. And I just love the story of how you met. We're so happy for you two."

"Yes," chimed in John. "And we'll leave the cake with you. We can pick up the plate later. It's only half-eaten."

Celia said nothing but tried to smile. Steve, however, rushed over to shake hands with the Vollmers.

"Wonderful that you could come by. It just wouldn't have been complete — and the cake was delicious."

Sarah and John waved at the others sitting in the living room and quickly exited out the front door, leaving behind them a hole in the conversation. Halfway down the walk to their car, which was parked on the street, John slipped his hand under Sarah's elbow and said lightly:

"I do agree it was time to leave, of course, but you made an awfully quick exit. Did you finish your study? Has Margaret Mead or her doppelganger reached any conclusions?"

"More than enough for tonight," she replied with a sudden serious tone in her voice, "more than enough, and I'm not sure they're terribly happy ones."

Inside the Watson house, the four remaining couples moved silently about the living room like mute players who had suddenly forgotten their lines. Teddy edged over to the bar to pour out another drink, and Celia ambled past Steve to sit next to Christine on the couch.

"Well, where were we?" said Dan, acting as prompter. "Oh, I know. We were talking about marriage. Well, I'd say that 20 years is quite a milestone — or did I mean millstone?"

"You would say something like that," said Marie. "At least when it comes to celebrating other people's anniversaries you're the life of the party."

"What's that supposed to mean?" Dan said, looking hurt. "Didn't I buy you a new car for your birthday — that 1955 Buick you wanted?"

"No, the Buick *you* wanted!" she replied quickly. "You scarcely even let me drive it. That's your trouble, Dan. The things you give people have a way of becoming your own possessions that can't be touched."

"Why, that's not fair at all. Haven't I...? No, I'm not going to say anything to defend myself. I don't have to. I just need another drink."

He walked over to where the bottles stood and poured out a large glass of scotch. He turned and glared at Marie and gestured with his drink in a faint ironic salute in her direction. Again, the room fell into an uncomfortable silence.

"Maybe we should think about going," said Jordan. "It's getting late."

"I think your dog can live without you for another hour," laughed Jim. "The party's not over yet."

"Well, there is something I'd like to ask all of you," broke in Christine, who seemed to be preoccupied and not listening attentively. "Teddy and I have been having a disagreement, and I thought maybe you all could help us decide."

"You mean support your position," interjected Teddy.

"Well, to be honest, yes. I thought our friends might have some sensible advice — something I rarely get at home." She paused for effect. "You see, Sandy wants to go on a summer trip sponsored by her college, to Europe — England, France and Italy. Chaperoned, of course, and I think it would just be wonderful, something I would have loved to do at her age. And travel is so much easier these days; they would cross in a week and land in London and then from there take the boat train to the Continent. I'm sure at least you would agree, Marie."

"And I say," interrupted Teddy, "that there's a darned sight better things to see here in the U.S. I don't understand all this talk about Europe and culture. Look at the mess they're still in. Why, some of those countries you mention are almost communist."

"There's no danger. You shouldn't be afraid, Teddy. A little adventure never hurt anyone," replied Christine.

"Me, afraid?" said Teddy, emphasizing the second word. "Afraid? Not likely. Not likely at all!"

"I think it's a wonderful idea," said Celia softly.

"And I do, too," added Jordan.

"Come on, fellows," cried Teddy. "What is this tonight, the battle of the sexes?"

"I'm afraid it's shaping up to be," replied Jim. "I'm with Teddy on this one. She'll have lots of time for adventure once she gets married."

"Now there's a twisted notion if I ever heard one!" exclaimed Jordan. "You've got it so wrong it's upside-down. Marriage is the end of adventure, not the beginning. It's all about obligations thereafter. When else would she have time to be on her own?"

"That's pretty bitter," said Dan. "I don't think you mean that, Jordan — speaking as your friend."

"And speaking as your wife," Marie broke in, "I'd say she's absolutely right. Now is the perfect time to go."

"I guess it's up to you to decide, then, Steve," said Teddy. "Do you support me on this one? After all, you know all about Italy from the war years."

Steve looked at Celia and said, somewhat sheepishly, "I guess I'll have to agree with you, Teddy. I saw some pretty awful things going on there. So yeah—"

"Agree with what?" cried Celia, standing suddenly. "That marriage ends any chance for adventure? Is that what you feel, that I'm some sort of stone around your neck, weighing you down, keeping you from the great adventures of life? Are you gasping for air and freedom from obligation, as Teddy so neatly puts it?"

"No, not that," Steve said angrily. "I was agreeing about the trip. I wouldn't want my daughter to go to Europe. It's not entirely safe for a girl, at least in my experience."

"You don't have a daughter," shot back Celia. "Couldn't have. And what experience are you talking about?"

"Damn it, Celia. It's not my problem, and you know it; we've had this argument for almost 20 years."

"Yes, it is, Steve. You know it is your fault that we don't have children," replied Celia, peering into her empty glass.

"Well, I guess the jury is divided on the trip," laughed Teddy. "We'll just have to sort it out ourselves." And then, looking around at the sullen faces of the group, he said merrily, "Let's all have another round and toast our hosts again."

"Hear! Hear!" exclaimed Dan, half-rising from his chair and then falling back. "I'll drink to that!"

"You'd drink to anything tonight," said Marie without expression.

There was another long pause. It seemed as if the room, despite the warm colors and bright lights, had suddenly become dim and cold.

Jim looked at all of them oddly, as if he were bursting with an idea that he could no longer contain, as if he had been waiting for this moment of hiatus.

"If you're all fortified, there is something I wanted to mention — something odd that I heard about. Just an idea, for the sake of conversation." He looked at Teddy, who seemed to be avoiding his glance.

Jordan eyed her husband with distaste, thinking that he was about to tell one of his long, complicated real estate stories about how he sold a property for a fortune that was nearer to collapse than of consequence.

"It's about an article I read in a magazine. Quite amazed me. I just couldn't imagine."

"What was it, Jim?" asked Celia politely.

"You don't want to know," Steve said quickly.

"But you know?" interrupted Celia. "What's this all about? Do you know, too, Teddy and Dan?"

"No doubt one of their tall tales about golf," said Jordan. "I caught them looking embarrassed and guilty the other day in the den during that rainstorm — after they abandoned their caddies out in the shelter.

"Not quite," said Jim. "But yes, I'll confess. I told them about this story I read in Esquire magazine."

"I don't think it's worth talking about, Jim. I warned you," said Dan, holding up his hand as if he were blocking an incoming snowball.

"Now you've got our attention," muttered Marie, looking puzzled and trying hard to concentrate. "Secrets for men only?"

"All right," Jim began. He spoke quickly: "I'll tell you. It's about a game called a key party. It's very simple and played with couples. Each wife puts her house key in a hat, and then every husband — not looking, of course, or feeling for a familiar edge — picks one out. And that's where he sleeps that night."

There was a sudden outburst of comments and excited voices, but Jordan hushed everyone.

"So that's what you were plotting the other day. I think you are all sick! Who would do such a thing? It's disgusting — adultery by Russian roulette, only every chamber loaded with a different dame."

"See? I told you not to bring it up," said Steve.

Jim looked helpless for a minute, until Marie suddenly spoke up.

"I'm curious," she said, looking around the room as if appraising the possibilities. "And just for the sake of conversation, I'd like to know how it works. For one, how would you know which key went with what house? And," she looked perplexed, "what are the chances you'd end up with your own husband? Wouldn't that be a disappointment?"

After a moment of silence, Christine laughed uncomfortably. "You're not serious, Marie. Who cares about the silly rules, since no one I know of is going to play that game?" She looked furiously at Teddy.

"There are rules," continued Jim. "At least that's what the article described. As I remember, here's what they are:

"One: Everyone has to agree to play.

"Two: Absolutely no discussion afterwards. No disclosure of partners, no gossip, no comparing notes and no notes taken.

"Three: Everything goes back to what it was before, as if nothing happened."

"But what about Marie's question?" insisted Jordan. "What are the chances you would just choose your own key and come home disappointed, having failed at your little scheme for a quick screw, just left standing there like the loser at musical chairs?"

"Odds are one in four. Not bad, actually," Jim said.

"And that we'd all end up with the same old partners?" chimed Marie.

"Highly unlikely!" Jim replied.

"Well," continued Jordan, "I think you're being really stupid, Jim, even to suggest such a thing. Think of the consequences."

"Oh, I don't know," Steve slurred, taking a hefty gulp of his drink.

Celia stood up and marched to stand in front of where he sat.

"How could you even think of such a thing on our anniversary?" she shouted down at him. She raised her hand as if to slap his face.

Steve answered without looking at her:

"It isn't our anniversary, actually. That was last week. And now we're already off and running into a new decade."

"You would do that to me?" she continued, her voice breaking like a wineglass shattering on a marble floor. "To me? After all I put up with from you? All right, damn you! I'll do it! I'm not your cautious, mousy little wife, but I'll be the whore you always tell everyone I am!" She began to sob.

"But, Jim," repeated Marie, completely ignoring this outburst, "answer me. How do you know which house key goes where?"

"You're really intrigued, aren't you, Marie?" exclaimed Dan. "You like the idea of sleeping around so long as there's community approval, don't you? There's a name for that!"

"And there's a name for you, too," she replied quickly. "Boring, domineering, possessive, self-important, uneducated. Oh, excuse me; that's several names. But they all fit, don't they?"

"So," continued Jim, unblinking, "we would tape a number to each key, and that would correspond to the name on a list. Simple enough to do."

Jim waved his arms around as if he were trying to lead an unruly orchestra of amateurs trying to play on the same beat and repeated: "Simple enough."

"Well, I, for one, say yes," said Marie defiantly. "What about you, Jordan? Christine? Shall we call the bluff of these schemers on their little plan, see if they're really serious about this game of promiscuous couples? I'm ready." She stood and stormed out into the front hallway. She had left her purse on the table by the front door. When she returned, she was holding a key.

"Here's my contribution!" And she flung it down on the ground. It bounced and then slid under the couch. Steve, who was sitting nearest to it, reached his hand under and pulled it out.

"Not so fast, Steve," laughed Jim. "No short circuits. If we're going to do this, we have to do it right."

Celia looked at Jim with such intensity that he turned away. "How can you talk about 'right' when you're planning to do such a despicable thing?" she said.

"What about the rest of the keys then?" asked Jim, undeterred.

Jordan and Christine stood up and walked out of the room and up the stairs leading to the master bedroom, where they had left their coats. Once there — and without a word — Jordan unsnapped her purse, which was lying on the bed, and picked out a key wallet, selecting the only brass-colored key. She quickly pressed it out of the small ring that held it.

Christine said suddenly, "I refuse to make this easy. If Teddy wants to play this game, he'll have to contribute his own key." She turned and led Jordan back down the stairs, gripping the bannister tightly to keep her balance.

"One more contribution to this nonsense," she said, swaying into the room. "But it won't be mine. You'll have to supply your key, Teddy, if you intend to go through with this. I'm leaving."

Teddy stood up, reached into his pocket, pulled out a key wallet and detached the key to his front door from the ring. He walked over deliberately and handed it to Jim, who also held Jordan's key.

"And now, Steve," said Jim, "we'll need a hat and some paper and Scotch tape to put a number on each key."

Celia looked at her husband in amazement, stunned by his apparent enthusiasm for this game. As she looked away again, she saw him, out of the corner of her eye, reaching into his pocket for their house key. He then stood and disappeared into the hall. In a moment, he returned with a gray fedora in his hand. Jim walked up to him and seized it, dropping three keys inside.

Steve hesitated a moment and then plunked his in, too.

"Now the paper and tape and we'll record the numbers on a separate sheet. As far as the game goes, the women can all go home now. And wait."

"Except me!" said Celia. "And I have to watch this? Look at the lascivious joy on all your faces! I think I'm beginning to enjoy this game; you're all so awful it's almost funny."

"No," said Steve sternly. "You go on upstairs."

"And wait for my knight in shining armor — the storybook ending to my marriage. This is so tawdry, even for you, Steve. It's really comical. And you with no sense of humor at all." She walked defiantly to the drinks table and poured a large glass of scotch. "This will be my best companion tonight!" she exclaimed, and she walked out of the room and tramped upstairs, followed by Christine, Marie and Jordan. When they had all assembled in the bedroom, Celia sat down abruptly on the edge of her bed.

"I won't hold it against any of you; I promise. But I want all of you to leave now. I have to face this alone."

Without a word, the other three women picked up all their things and then walked downstairs. Without even glancing into the living room, Jordan called out. "We're all going home. And we'll be taking the cars. Wherever you're going, gentlemen, you can make your way on foot."

As they stepped out the door, Jordan slammed it shut.

The four men sat in the living room without uttering a word. The atmosphere had somehow thickened with a heavy lurid light, with a floating residue of cigarette smoke hanging in a low cloud over everything. Jim was the first to speak:

"I'm a bit amazed. I never thought this would happen and that they would go through with it."

"Yes, you did," Dan insisted. "You planned this. You orchestrated everything. You made it into a game of chicken, and now everyone is afraid to back out."

"But I really didn't," insisted Jim. "I thought all along that our wives would say no, and now we have all convinced ourselves. It's too late to turn back. At first, I thought they agreed out of anger or revenge — surely not desire."

"What's the difference at our age?" said Dan.

"I'm not sure you're right," said Teddy. "I watched their faces, and despite the protest and shock, I really think they were almost eager. It surprises me, and I'm not going to ask why. But it sure is a revelation — because, after all, any one of them could have put a wrench into the whole thing and yet no one did. Yes, I think they want to play. They want a bit of adventure, I guess. Well, if they do, I do, too."

"You may be right," said Jim. "So let's get on with it. Steve, you write down numbers from one to four on scraps of paper and tape them to the keys. Then everyone can identify their key and put the name on a master list. And then we'll choose."

When Steve had finished this task and the names were entered on the list, he dropped the keys into the hat.

"I'll go first," he said, "since I'm the host."

"Not so fast," said Jim. "Just a reminder: No conversation about this tomorrow or ever. No one should ever know. I'll hold the hat then."

Steve approached and thrust his hand into the hat. Clutching the key in the palm of his hand like a secret talisman, he walked to the dining room table, where the list had been placed, and glanced at the names written down. Teddy and Dan followed suit, leaving the last key for Jim.

"I think it's best if we leave one by one," he said. "No further conversation. You go first, why don't you, Dan. Everyone gets a five-minute head start."

Chapter 8

Dan pressed the key in his pocket, running his finger over the cut-out slots and teeth. He headed up the street toward his house and Jim Reilly's. When he arrived, he saw the big cream and red Buick Roadmaster resting in the driveway like a tired circus wagon, its intricate lines and vivid colors reflected in the gleam of the street lamp. There was a single light in the living room, and he knew that it created a semi-dark atmosphere. Was she sitting quietly waiting for her surprise lover, with the lights turned low to set a romantic mood? he wondered. He looked across the street to his own house. It was shrouded in black and gray shadows. If he tried to enter the Reillys' house with the key he had chosen, he knew he would stumble around in the dark and make a fool of himself. And no doubt the dog would go crazy at the intrusion. Jordan could wait for him, he thought, and anyway, he was curious to see who had chosen the key to his house — and to Marie. So he positioned himself behind the large holly bush that bordered the steps and landing of the front door and crouched down low and out of sight to wait.

It seemed like a very long time until he finally heard the scuff of footfalls on the road. At first, the shape was only a dim outline, but as it grew larger, Dan recognized first the gait and then the shape of his neighbor Jim, who was making for the walkway leading to the front door. Jim stopped for a moment and looked around and then glanced at the key he held in his hand. Suddenly, he had begun to move again, along the brick walk. His steps were quieter now, as if he were sneaking up to the house. When he reached the landing, he stopped again and looked around, out into the featureless black night. Fixing his gaze on the door, he aimed the key at the lock.

"I had a suspicion it would be you," Dan exclaimed, stepping out from behind the bush. "In fact, I was sure you'd rig the game somehow. You're pretty easy to read, old friend. I think I know you rather well by now. Your mysteries are only a bunch of obvious clues."

"What?" Jim blurted out. "What are you doing here, Dan? This isn't part of the game. Where are you supposed to be?"

"Right here," said Dan fiercely. "This is my house and my car and my wife. I've every right."

"But the rules..."

"Damn your rules, Jim. I've suspected all along that this was going to be a setup. This smells of a plot. You've always wanted to fuck my wife. I've watched you. In fact, you've probably tried already — maybe even succeeded — and that's why she agreed so quickly to the game, hoping you'd win. Maybe even rigged! So isn't this just a cover for your affair?" Dan edged closer to Jim, standing only inches from his face, and continued:

"So why don't you just run along home now? Game's over. Here's your key if you need a spare." Saying this, he reached out and pulled Jim away from the front door, almost tripping him.

"Take your hands off me, Dan. You've got it all wrong. And don't push me," he said, grabbing Dan's sleeve to keep from falling.

Dan shoved him again and threw down his key. It clattered and then disappeared into the grass. "And if I ever see you hanging around here again," he said, "you'll pay for it!"

"Screw you!" exclaimed Jim. "You're sick and jealous. Here's your key back then."

He reached out abruptly and pushed the key in Dan's face, brushing his cheek as he did.

Dan grabbed his hand, wrenched the key out and then gave him a powerful shove. Jim cried out and tried to catch his balance but flew instead into the holly bush and then crashed onto the sidewalk.

"You bastard!" he cried. "What the hell have you done? I'm sure I broke something!"

Just then, the porch lights went on, and Dan's eldest son appeared at the door in his pajamas, trying to comprehend the scene in front of him.

"Mr. Reilly," he exclaimed. "What happened? Are you hurt? I can see a lot of blood on your face. Dad, what's going on?"

"I think I've broken my nose," Jim whined.

"Go get a towel, son," said Dan, "and we'll clean up this mess. I'll drive you to the hospital, Jim — if there really is something broken and you're not just faking." He added: "Stupid game! Stupid night! And don't even think about bleeding on my leather seats!"

~~~

Teddy stood in the shadows halfway up the block. The cloudless night was intensely dark, as no moon appeared, and the stars were just small gems sewn onto black velvet and cast little light. As his eyes became more accustomed to the dark, he could make out the trees that lined the road and, a hundred yards away, the lights of the Watson house, which shone with a warm orange glow. Across the street he could also make out the mass of his own house, sitting like an animal at rest, with the twin porch lights its gleaming, shuttered eyes. He stood off the road in a secluded spot because he was waiting for Steve to emerge and walk toward his destination. Teddy had drawn Celia's key and could only double back when Steve had left. As he stood, he thought about the folly of this absurd game, its careful rules and its careless potential to disrupt and destroy. Why, he asked himself, had he agreed in the first place? Why wasn't he stronger and a leader instead of always being a yes man among his quartet of friends. What puzzled him most was Christine's agreement to play. Was she as bored — and now he stopped to think about that word — was she as bored with marriage as he was? Was there nothing left to anticipate in life or to aspire to? They had moved to Golf View Court, which had always seemed to him like a dream outside of possibility. And Christine had made that possible with her inheritance. But then what — the endless rounds of seasons and golf matches that only reminded him of his thwarted ambition and the injury that had spoiled his career as a professional? How had it happened that the games they all played — and this one, too — were more real somehow than anything else? Was life just a downward spiral from now on into make-believe while time only increased his golf handicap — yes, handicap, an apt metaphor for a future of hooks and slices? He almost chuckled out loud at his sudden insight. The signs of aging weren't just wrinkles and the day-after sore knees and shoulders from swinging a golf club or even the decline in his sex drive. It was the slow rise of his handicap, the surest measure of his age and his ability to compete. He wasn't even sure which made him more bitter, lousy golf scores and duffed shots or his steadily diminishing interest in sex. Perhaps that was what had motivated him tonight — seeing the game as a restoration of something, as a way of pushing back against the inexorable and jumping out of the groove of habit. But suddenly, he was feeling what he desired most every night, simply to sleep in his own bed, stretch out and touch the warmth of his wife. And the last thing he wanted was Celia or Marie or Jordan. As he watched intently, a sudden breeze shifted the branches of the trees above him, making him so dizzy as he watched them that he almost fell to the ground. He was drunk — on self-pity and Steve Watson's anniversary booze.

Having waited almost 10 minutes and now feeling more jittery and foolish than ever, Teddy wondered whether the headlights of a passing car might spotlight him and hold him up to suspicion. He knew that no one walked out at this late hour, at least no one who actually belonged on Golf View Court, so he turned and headed back down the street. When he reached the point where his driveway and the Watsons' faced each other in two broad scoops, he stopped for a moment, and then he turned toward his own house. He could see now that the living room lights were on. Whoever was there, he would deal with it, but for him, the game was over.

As he entered the unlocked door, he heard voices coming from the living room. He purposely shut the door with an exaggerated thrust and stamped his feet on the throw rug, as if to shed imaginary moisture or mud, before he walked down the hall and into the room.

"I hope I'm not interrupting something," he exclaimed sarcastically as he swung into the room.

"How the hell could you?" shot Christine's voice. "It's your own house, Teddy."

What he saw surprised him. Christine was sitting on the leather armchair, still wearing her party dress, now wrinkled and creased. She had removed her shoes and tucked one leg under her. Her face had a drawn and exhausted look that her makeup, as if it had been applied to each single feature with a different and conflicting purpose, now exaggerated. Teddy could see, despite her lack of energy, that she was furious, and his appearance only brought a renewed scowl.

"So the famous golf pro slinks home," she said. "Did you score?"

"Oh, Christine," he exclaimed.

"Get me a drink, Teddy. And while you're at it, something for Steve."

Teddy hesitated and then looked to Steve, who was sitting hunched over in the middle of the sofa, his legs spread and a forearm resting on each knee. He looked up and nodded as if he had just been casually introduced to the town bore.

"Make mine a scotch, if you don't mind, Teddy," he said. "But not too strong. I've had more than my share tonight."

Teddy walked into the dining room and picked three glasses from the liquor cabinet and opened the bottle of scotch. In the kitchen, he found a half-full ice tray in the freezer compartment of the refrigerator and put two meager cubes in each glass, pouring out a two-jigger drink for each. Finding no convenient tray, he gripped all three glasses in his hands and walked carefully back to the living room.

"You'll spill if you don't watch out," said Christine.

"Don't care much if I do," he mumbled, doling out the drinks to each of them. He took a seat in a chair at the other end of the room, facing Christine. "And no," he exclaimed, "I didn't score."

"Is that regret I hear," she said, glaring at him, "or just the admission, you know, that you couldn't perform? Wouldn't be the first time..." Her voice trailed off.

Teddy almost winced but chose to ignore the anger in her voice.

"I drew Steve's key. Here it is," he said, reaching into his pocket. "And I decided this was just a crazy, drunken impulse. Somehow we all let drink and Jim's cajoling convince us to do something really dangerous. I don't know. Maybe wife swapping is for some people, if it ever actually happens, but not me. And I can see that you two are still downstairs. Is this just the courtship phase or the afterwards — the detumescence? And yes, I'm not as stupid as you think I am. I know a few big words."

"From reading pornography, no doubt," said Christine, scarcely able to contain her scorn.

Steve sat up and took a sip from the drink Teddy had given him.

"You've got everything wrong, Teddy," he began, "or maybe in your confused way, you've got it right. Anyway, Christine and I were just talking, trying to figure out how we had all gotten into such a crazy mood. As if we were all struck by the need to prove something and find some lost and dimming vitality. I guess I'm upset about being married for 20 years and thinking of the next 20 and then... And Celia wanting so badly to have a daughter or even a son, that I can't give her. At least you have Sandy. I guess I'd give almost anything to be able to fight with my wife over the summer plans of our own flesh and blood. Except that we can't. And you can't imagine the silences.

Of course, we have our social life, but how could that substitute? A dog like Jordan's? You can't imagine the quietness after dinner. There's nothing we can talk about that we made together. I mean, what do you say to each other? 'How was your day, dear?' How can I explain my day? It's always just seeing the same clients and solving the same problems. Oh, a decision is necessary here and there, but is it interesting to anyone but me? And her day? Should I inquire about doing the dishes and shopping and the laundry and listening to soap operas on the radio or reading a romance novel?"

"You could ask her how she feels, couldn't you?" said Christine, looking at Teddy.

"You mean if she has a headache or something?"

"No, of course not," replied Christine. "What I mean is a serious discussion, not about things but about emotions. I'm sure you know what I mean."

"Not entirely, no, but I think I'd be too embarrassed."

"And you're not embarrassed now — you and Teddy wanting to commit adultery behind the facade of 'everyone's doing it, so why not me'? I think you men are pretty pathetic seeking public approval for your affairs."

"But," broke in Teddy, "Christine, you agreed to it."

"Yes, I said 'yes,' and I think for a moment, I was really intrigued. But now I understand that I meant 'no' from the beginning. You see, I must have had this sudden, overwhelming urge to test you, to see how far you would go. And now I know."

"But, Christine, I didn't go anywhere except halfway up the block and then back home. I was supposed to go back to Celia's and Steve's, but you see, I didn't; I couldn't."

"And so being a coward makes you heroic? What do you want me to say?"

After a long pause, Steve stood up and smoothed out his slacks with one hand. He took a final gulp of his drink and then set the glass down on the coffee table in front of the sofa.

"I guess I'll head home now," he said. "Celia will be wondering since no one has showed up. It's time to end the party." Neither Teddy nor Christine said a word, and Steve walked alone out into the hall and then through the front door and out across the two driveways.

~~~

Dan sat in the pink fiberglass chair, shifting his weight with discomfort and fingering the aluminum tubes that served as armrests. Glancing around the emergency waiting room, he saw several patients, a few who seemed merely drunk and one elderly woman whose face looked like bleached parchment, her eyes sunken and clouded with cataracts and her loose, thin curls revealing the rough pink skin of her scalp. Not moving, she seemed content simply to wait. No one looked as obviously injured as Jim had been. He had moaned and complained all the way to the hospital and then had to be bundled into a wheelchair. Dan had signed him in and promised to remain for a diagnosis. But that hadn't prevented Jim from shouting a parting salvo at him as he was escorted through the swinging doors into the treatment area: "I'll sue you, you bastard. Just wait and see. And I don't give a damn if you are a lawyer; you're going to pay for assaulting me!"

Dan had left the bloody towel in the trunk of his car. In a way, he was grateful that Jim's injury was serious enough — on the surface, at least — that he demanded to be driven to Suburban Hospital immediately rather than to the police station. Dan knew, of course, that any legal recourse of Jim's would be folly. After all, he was defending his property against a home invasion. But the embarrassment and scandal of any follow-up would be disastrous for him. As he sat in the over-bright room — with its shining linoleum floor, pastel walls and Norman Rockwell reproductions hanging two to each side of the room — he could imagine the shocked looks on the faces of his law partners if they heard about the key party. Even those who were jealous and intrigued would join their tut-tuts of disapproval to the general chorus of condemnation. And no matter what did or did not happen, gossip would move around the firm, creating a story that, if he denied it, would only multiply into competing rumors like shrapnel from an explosion of innuendo and accusation. He doubted that he could survive that, so he would have to persuade Jim, as well as the others, to keep quiet.

Such thoughts made him so restless that he stood up abruptly and began to pace back and forth, his shoes squeaking on the heavily waxed linoleum floor. The only person to watch him was the nurse who sat behind a desk that guarded the door leading to the intake area. Finally, exasperated at his nervousness, she said firmly:

"Please sit down, sir. You are disturbing the others. We will get to you soon."

"I'm not the patient," said Dan, stopping in front of her desk. "I'm waiting for Jim Reilly. I already signed him in over an hour ago. I'm his friend, and I brought him here. I've been waiting to find out how badly he's injured. His wife will want to know as soon as possible.

"All right, Mr....?"

"Clements," he added, although for a moment, he was tempted to give a false name.

"Mr. Clements, if they know you're here, I'm sure you will be notified. But please do sit down now," she growled.

~~~

Steve walked slowly down Teddy Barr's driveway and across the street. He felt miserable, and his head ached, and he was unsure of the source of the almost physical disquiet that was beginning to gather in his chest — a shortness of breath that alarmed him. Was it an incipient hangover coming on or shame or guilt or, he wondered, the emptiness left over from unsatisfied excitement and desire that had scooped an emotionally hollow feeling in him? Or was he simply exhausted? The lights of his house were still on, and when he entered the living room, everything remained in disorder and hasty abandonment — furniture slightly out of place, half-empty glasses strewn about on tables, with some on the floor. Visible under the archway of the dining room was the long table that held the remains of the potluck dinner — casserole dishes, serving plates encrusted with food, crumpled napkins and the partially eaten chocolate cake, looking like the ruin of a besieged castle, its structure undermined and broken.

"God, what a mess!" he mumbled as he retreated to the hallway. And Celia hadn't even begun to clear it up. He promised himself he would help her in the morning. He paused for a moment before starting up the stairs, looking into the darkness at the top. And then he began to climb — carefully because he felt woozy and tired. When he reached the top, he saw that the master bedroom door was closed. He approached it quietly and listened. Perhaps, he thought, Celia was already asleep, and he imagined for a moment slipping silently into her bed and wrapping his arms around her warm body. But then he stopped, because she might, in fact, be waiting expectantly for whoever had drawn their house key. Taking a step forward, he grasped the door handle and turned it gently, and then he pushed to open it. It seemed to be stuck, so he pushed harder, until he realized that something heavy was leaning against the other side.

"Celia," he called softly. "Celia, it's Steve."

"You? You? Go away," he heard her cry.

"Come on, Celia, it's your husband; let me in."

"I don't give a damn who you are! And especially not you. Leave me alone. Go back to your new mistress!"

"Celia, please, I'm sorry. Nothing happened, honestly," he exclaimed.

"You're wrong!" she shouted. "Everything has happened! Now go away! I never want to see you again!"

Steve put his ear against the door and heard her sobbing. He pushed again, hard this time, and heard a scraping sound as the chest of drawers, which she had somehow managed to drag across the room to block the entrance, moved a couple of inches.

"Stay out of here! Don't you dare come near me!" she called, the pitch of her voice rising almost to a scream. "Out!"

He realized that it was foolish to try further, with nothing to be gained by shouting through a blockaded wooden door, so he retreated to the spare bedroom down the hall. Entering it, he sat down on the bed in the dark, with only the dim illumination of the hallway casting orange shadows in the room. He reached down, untied his shoes and kicked them off. He would not remember, the next morning, when he had finally stretched out on the bed, nor could he recall any dreams. But the oblivion of the terrible night had returned with a jolt the moment he awoke and realized where he was.

~~~

Gradually, the emergency room emptied, until only Dan and the nurse remained. Around 1 a.m., the door behind her swished open, and an orderly emerged. He leaned down and spoke to her in low tones, hand cupped over his mouth. When he finished, he stood straight, and she looked at Dan and gave a nod of her head.

"You can see him now," she conceded. "Just follow the orderly here. He'll take you back."

"Thank you," Dan said, trying to be as polite as he could for fear that she might suddenly change her mind. It was, he thought, appalling to be at the whim of such a petty tyrant, whose stiff white uniform gave her the power to command or dismiss his presence.

Once inside the hospital corridor, the orderly led Dan past several brightly lighted treatment rooms and then around a corner and into what was obviously the patient area. The smell of antiseptic sharpened the atmosphere. Standing in front of one of the hospital rooms was a doctor waiting for them to arrive.

Dan stretched out his hand as he approached, but the doctor just nodded his head, giving him a diffident look.

"Your friend is finally resting. You can see him for a moment. He's lucky; it looked a lot worse than it was. But he's got a broken nose and a concussion, so we're going to keep him overnight for observation. He said something about his wife, and I suppose you can let her know. Five minutes, and no excitement."

"Thank you, Dr....?"

"We will release him tomorrow sometime after noon." With this brief amendment, the doctor retreated down the hallway, although the orderly remained, presumably to guard against a prolonged visit. Dan wondered whether Jim had said anything about how his injuries had occurred. That might explain the obvious unfriendliness of everyone, unless, of course, this was simply standard late-night hospital etiquette.

Dan walked into the room. There were two beds, one unoccupied, with a drawn curtain between them. Jim lay quietly, propped up by several pillows. He was dressed in a short-sleeved pastel blue hospital gown. His arms, resting outside the sheet, were blotched with red welts and scratches, and his face had two bandages — a strip of gauze wound tightly around his forehead and a large white pad covering his nose and taped in place by strips of adhesive that extended across his cheeks, almost to his ears.

Dan approached cautiously, patting the bed when he reached it.

"Look, Jim," he began, "I'm really sorry. None of this was intentional; it's just rotten luck."

"The only rot around here," mumbled Jim, "is your temper. I've a mind to sue you."

"Wouldn't hold up in court. You know that," he said dismissively. "But look, I'm not here to argue, just to make sure you're OK. I'll go back right now to Golf View and tell Jordan. She'll be wondering — and worried. And you just let me know if there's anything else I can do."

"Bastard," said Jim, whose eyes seemed to show delight in his power to intimidate Dan. "Wait till everyone hears about this."

"I don't think this is a story any of us want told around, Jim. We'd have to say whose idea it was. And honestly, it's all best forgotten. Can't imagine what folks would think."

"Easy enough for you to say."

"Yes, I suppose it is, but just get some rest. We'll talk about it later."

"Maybe," said Jim, closing his eyes.

Dan interpreted this as a sign for him to leave.

"Goodbye. I'm on my way to talk to Jordan."

"Just don't exaggerate," said Jim suddenly. "I don't want her showing up here tonight, distraught and full of tears and making a big show of things. I've had enough drama to last a long time."

"OK. I'll try."

Dan walked out of the room and into the corridor, nodding to the orderly who had been keeping watch. Following the exit sign, he found himself at the front entrance. The floodlit front parking lot was deserted except for his Buick and two other cars. When he reached his car and opened the door, he peered into the interior, examining it by the dull illumination of the overhead bulb. Immediately, he saw a large dark stain on the white leather on the passenger side. He cursed silently and slid into the driver's seat. He was almost tempted to drive straight home and ignore Jordan entirely. Let the Reillys stew, for all he cared. But as he approached the turnoff to Golf View Court, he edged into their driveway and got out of the car. He knocked loudly at the door. Jordan answered immediately.

"How is he?" she asked.

"So you know."

"Yes, Marie came over right after you left for the hospital. Your boy told her what happened."

"He's OK, Jordan. A slight concussion and a broken nose and some bruises and cuts."

"Did you do all that?" she asked.

"No. He fell. They're keeping him for observation. Should get out around noon tomorrow. He said he didn't want you to come, and not to worry."

"I'm too angry at the rat to worry about him. I wish you had punched him, Dan. This was all his idea, and look where it's gotten us and him."

As she spoke, Marie appeared from the house across the street. She had changed into a plain dress and low-heeled shoes, as if she had purposely dressed down for the occasion.

"Let's go home, Dan," she said as she approached, grabbing his arm. "Jordan's OK now that she knows he'll live."

"Yes," repeated Jordan, her voice surcharged with unfriendliness and fatigue. "Just go home."

Marie turned around and led Dan up their driveway. When they reached the landing of the front door, she stopped and pulled at his arm.

"You did it, didn't you?" she said. "I was sure you were fighting."

"I just pushed him, nothing more, and then he fell. Except I guess I helped him a bit."

"Good," said Marie abruptly. "You're not forgiven, but that's a start."

~~~

No one noticed when Jim and Jordan Reilly returned from the hospital the next day, although Dan Clements saw that their car was missing around noon. It was better unremarked, he thought, as if ignoring the return of the Golf View wounded warrior would somehow erase everything that had happened. He and Marie had stayed up late talking, pretending that the harsh words that had passed between them earlier could somehow be resolved into mutual understanding. It had been, even in his condition, a sobering and harrowing few hours, and the aftertaste of her bitter recriminations and accusations still remained, even if her temper had abated. That next morning, Marie had risen early and dressed in a smart business suit. She woke Dan with an unfriendly shove and demanded that he drive her to the station. Sitting on a towel covering the stained seat of the Buick, she looked out the window as if the familiar passing houses and lawns were a fresh and unknown landscape that fascinated her.

"Meet me this afternoon," she demanded as he stopped in front of the entrance. "I'll be on the 3:58 from downtown." She pivoted out, stood and then slammed the door. In an instant, she had disappeared into the interior of the station. Although she said nothing about her precise destination and probably wouldn't have told him even if he'd asked, Dan knew she would spend the day at Field's or wherever else she had a charge account. He would have to wait until the beginning of next month when the bills came in to see the measure of her anger. She hadn't bothered to ask whether there would be a golf game that afternoon, but given Jim's condition, it was obvious there wouldn't be. And in any case, she had made it apparent that her plans would come first. The only instructions she had given him regarded lunch for the boys. He could make them cold chicken sandwiches or tinned deviled ham — whatever he wanted; she didn't care.

~~~

At the Watson house, Steve took a long shower in the spare bathroom and then slipped on his slacks and undershirt and went downstairs. He didn't bother trying his bedroom door again. Working carefully — because he wanted to make as little noise as possible — he collected and washed the dishes, straightened the furniture and opened the front door to air out the house. The day was cool and bright, and it made him nervous and jittery that he wasn't playing golf right then. He couldn't imagine that anyone in the foursome would show up. But as he worked, he convinced himself that a day outdoors would do him good, even if he couldn't play with his regulars. And besides, he had earned his leave and, he hoped, Celia's forgiveness by cleaning up the house.

When he was ready to leave, Celia remained in the bedroom, still barricaded, he assumed. So he left a note propped against the sugar dish on the kitchen table:

"I've gone to the club. Back around 6:00. How can I tell you how sorry I am? Love, Steve."

Chapter 9

Arriving at the club around midday, Steve Watson waited in the locker room with his caddie until the greens master found him a threesome that was only playing nine holes. He was happy enough to join them, although he felt miserable and played only well enough to keep up with the others. When the group swung around to the fifth hole and began to play parallel to Golf View Court, he felt extremely tense and even lost a ball in the woods after a long, wild drive off the sixth tee. After stamping around and kicking up clumps of fallen leaves, he agreed to take a penalty shot. There was no point in retrieving it, he thought, as the mere idea of retrieving anything made him anxious. Even his caddie caught his insouciant mood and declined to give him any encouragement. When the group finally finished the front nine, Steve left the threesome and walked to the terrace for a drink, hoping that more poison in his system would be an antidote for the discomfort he felt. The afternoon was still warm, but a damp wave rose from the fairways and gardens around the clubhouse. It would not be long, he sighed, before golf would be impossible for another year. There were a few players who went out even in November and early December, but he hated the cold, hard ground and the tricky winds and the way the ball skittered across the greens; he hated the chill that forced him to wear heavy clothes that impeded what was already an ineffectual swing. And anyway, he thought, the foursome with whom he had played so many rounds had probably splintered forever into angry singles looking for other partners.

As he approached the terrace, he caught sight of Mrs. Smith, her bronze legs set off by long dark cutoff pants. Her blond hair was swept back in a silk scarf as if she were just about to embark on a convertible ride. There was a man sitting at her table, and Steve immediately recognized the thin, sloping shoulders of Dan Clements. They both had highball glasses in front of them. When Mrs. Smith caught and held Steve's eye for a moment, Dan turned and, seeing who it was, gave him a look that dissolved into the hostile glare of warning that one might give to a menacing stranger. So Steve turned away. His own eyes had grown cold at this curt dismissal, and he wanted nothing more than to change out of his golf cleats and head home. But he did wonder about Mrs. Smith. What was her game? And what was Dan telling her?

When he arrived at his house, he pulled in to the driveway and stopped. He glanced, as he almost always did, through the eye-level windows of the garage and noticed that Celia's car was missing. Once inside the house, he headed straight to the kitchen, hoping to find some explanation. But there was nothing — only his own communication lying against the sugar dish where he had left it, apparently unread.

"Celia," he called, backing out into the hall and projecting his voice upstairs. "Are you home?"

He knew, of course, that she was not, but he climbed upstairs anyway to the bedroom to check. The door was half-open, so he entered tentatively.

"Celia," he said again. There was nothing, however, but the aura of vacated emotion. The bedclothes were in disarray, and the dresser was not yet back in its accustomed place. He walked around the room, looked out the window that opened onto the driveway and then turned again. He noticed that the closet door stood partially open. When he moved to shut it, he saw a large empty space along the hanger bar where Celia's clothes normally hung. As if to confirm what he now knew, he rushed out to the hall closet, where the suitcases were kept. Two of the larger ones were missing, and the others were tumbled as if someone — Celia — had dragged them out and then jammed them back in in anger. He returned to the bedroom and spread the crumpled sheets and blankets back toward the headboard of her bed, arranged the pillows and sat down, leaning against them.

"Not even a note," he said out loud.

He was scarcely conscious of the time he remained in this position. He finally roused himself to go downstairs when he realized that some of the discomfort he felt was not grief but hunger. In the kitchen, he opened the refrigerator and stood looking, but not really focusing on the carefully wrapped bags of fruit and vegetables and the neatly stacked glass and plastic containers. Finally, he reached for a jar of peanut butter and a bottle of milk. There was a loaf of white bread in the breadbox on the counter, and he took out two slices and slathered them, adding some strawberry jam from a pot he found on the kitchen table. He sat down and thought about what he ought to do. Celia had undoubtedly gone to her sister's home in Winnetka; he was not worried about her in that respect. What troubled him was the two of them — as a couple — and not knowing whether they could ever overcome the terrible botched anniversary party. His meager and tasteless meal fit his celibate and self-pitying mood. He found himself musing about his life and his marriage, but he was only able, he realized after a while, to think of it in the past tense. He vividly remembered the early years of excitement and joy, although he knew that even if he judged their marriage a success in those days, the intensity was only a fast-burning candle. When had the light gone out? He couldn't say, for it was not a single snuffing-out of the warmth but a slow wearing of life into grooves of routine that had brought him to this state. The daily grind, he thought. Perhaps it would have been different if he had been able to give her a child, the daughter that she yearned for as desperately as if it were a lost child she grieved and not just an idea and a hope. When had her longing become mourning for someone who never existed? Notwithstanding his words last night, he knew it was his fault; the doctor had explained it to him after he underwent several tests. Completely his fault, yet he always blamed her anyway — and publicly.

Despite this failing, their partnership at least had become comfortable, like an old shirt, yet so worn that it was on the edge of becoming frayed at every point of stress. Maybe, he thought, that's what had motivated him last night, in his self-destructive mood, thinking that some single cruel act could suddenly jolt them both out of their ennui. Maybe now, he thought, she would stay away long enough that they could somehow re-create the imagination of each other that only absence could foster and that would allow them to fall in love again with the idea of love. But right now, all he could think was that he was content to be alone, except that he vowed this would be his last peanut butter dinner. Most meals, he knew, he would have to eat out. Not at the club, because that would provoke too many questions, but he could drive to the next town, where there were several restaurants. It would be slow and a waste of time and a bother to eat alone, but what else did he have to do until she returned?

As he sat meditating on his sorry self, with his sense of resentment and grievance mounting, he became surer than ever that he was the injured party. Leaving was overly dramatic; just like her to pull something like that.

Just as anger had begun to replace his shame, he heard the chimes of the front doorbell. Reluctantly, he got up and walked into the hallway, turning on the porch light as he did. It would not be Celia yet. She would certainly wish to make her absence longer than one uncomfortable afternoon. And besides, she had her own key. He was puzzled. When he opened the door, he saw it was Teddy.

"Hi, Steve," Teddy began. "Can't come in. Just stopped by to give you a message. Celia just called Christine and asked her to let you know she's at her sister's place."

Steve knew, of course, but he was still surprised that she had chosen to communicate in this roundabout fashion.

"Do you want to come in for a minute?" he asked.

"No, I really can't," Teddy answered. "I'm sorry. Just carrying out orders. Can't stay. And not really sure I want to. You look awful, Steve. Get some rest."

"Yeah, I feel..." he started and then stopped. "But you know. Anyway, thanks."

Teddy turned around and hastened down the two porch steps of the landing and then along the path across the lawn that led to the street. Steve watched him hurry and felt almost sorry for a minute that his friend had become a go-between in his marital problems with Celia. Closing the door, he turned off the porch light and went back into the kitchen to rinse off his plate and glass.

~~~

In Winnetka, Celia and her sister, Marge, sat in the breakfast alcove in the kitchen. Marge's husband had long since been dismissed — and happily so for him, because he realized that he wanted nothing to do with their conversation. Instead, he sat with his daughter in the upstairs bedroom while she struggled with her algebra homework.

"Are you going to call him tonight?" quizzed Marge.

"No," replied Celia. "Telling the neighbor was enough; he'll get the message."

"Won't he worry?"

"I certainly hope he will, but probably not, and I'm past caring about his feelings. I'm just sick and tired of him and of my whole life. He has hurt me so often I'm just covered with scars. All this time, I've been like a mouse, and I'm sick of it and of myself. What has happened to me? I have nothing to show for those 20 married years except a torn-up diary of hopes. I don't want to be the timid, frigid Celia anymore, the washed-up housewife in her faded housedress that everyone pities. And I blame him. Not just for last night, but I'm beginning to see, clearly—"

"Well, you know," Marge interrupted, "that I've never really liked him very much. I didn't say anything at the time, but—"

"Oh, you made it plain enough. Just don't tell me now that you had some sort of premonition. It's my problem, and I'll deal with it my own way."

"But it's terrible what those men tried to do, so drunk and disloyal on your anniversary," Marge continued.

"It wasn't our actual anniversary," corrected Celia sternly.

"Well, near enough; and you know what I mean."

"Yes, I do. But let me be angry for myself. This isn't your battle, and don't interfere. I'm trying to find the strength to deal with it myself, and you're not helping me by telling me, 'I told you so' — when in fact, you didn't say a word. In fact, I always thought you assumed he was too good for me!" Celia looked angrily at Marge and then wiped a tear from her eyes with the wadded-up and damp handkerchief she gripped in her fist.

"But you shouldn't be hasty," continued Marge, determined to give advice. "Decisions made in anger—"

"I may be angry and hurt and feeling reckless, Marge, but I'm actually feeling something for the first time in a long while. And don't try to talk me out of it. I just need to find the courage to act. I know I'm not strong enough to go back and fight with him. He'd win with a few sweet words, and then I'd be back to being the same dull housewife! Don't you see? Running away is the only thing I can do to save myself!"

"So you really are going to speak to a lawyer?"

"Yes," said Celia defiantly. "And I think I'll use that downtown firm — Temple and Scowcroft. I'm sure they have someone competent who can handle divorces."

"But aren't they very expensive?"

"Oh, I'm sure they are. Top-of-the-line. One of our neighbors is a partner, Dan Clements."

"That name sounds familiar. Wasn't he one of the men at your party? I think you said there were four couples."

"Yes, he was there. And I can just picture his face when he sees shy little Celia sitting in the office of one of his partners. He'll know for sure that when I tell my story, it'll get back to him."

"But don't lawyers keep the secrets of their clients?"

"I've heard that. Like priests. But not this secret. Anyway, I want it to get out. I have grounds to take everything — the house, Steve's bank account, alimony.."

Pronouncing the last word, Celia began sobbing. "Everything if I have the courage!"

~~~

On Wednesday evening, Sarah Vollmer finished washing the dishes. Wiping her hands on the French linen tapestry cloth she kept hanging by the stove, she looked out into the darkness. The days were getting shorter now, she thought, and soon standard time would hasten nightfall even earlier. From the living room, she could hear the exuberant andante movement of Tchaikovsky's Symphony No. 5, John's favorite. She turned, resolute, and walked to the cabinet at the opposite end of the kitchen. Leaning over, she pulled out a bottle of Grand Marnier from the bottom shelf and then straightened to reach for the glasses that sat at eye level. She clasped two small green-stemmed crystal goblets in the fingers of one hand, letting them clink musically against each other. Setting them down, she tipped two small portions of the golden liquid into the glasses and then carried them carefully into the living room. Without a word, she handed one to her husband and then sat down opposite him on the couch. As the music came to its triumphal end, she plunged the tip of her tongue into the thick liquid and savored its cloying sweetness.

When the music finally stopped and the room fell silent, John sat up straight in his easy chair.

"I've been reading about new record players and microphones and speakers," he said, half to himself. "The new recordings will now be double-grooved, not like these old ones, with part of the sound conveyed to one speaker and a part to the other so that it gives the impression of three dimensions — just like the ears, as well as the eyes, work."

"But won't you have to buy all new records then?" asked Sarah.

"Absolutely — and a completely new sound system; that's the beauty of it. I'm going into Chicago to the Merchandise Mart next week to listen to a demonstration. It will be wonderful for business and a whole new experience, new equipment, a new stereophonic world. That's the name of the process.

"That seems extraordinary, John. But what about your collection? You have so many records you enjoy already, and you worked so hard to build it up."

"I won't get rid of them, ever. Still, I'm excited to know if it works as well as the promotional literature says."

Sarah nodded but went silent while he stared at her. After a minute or so, John put down his glass and made a slight grimace.

"I know that look on your face," he said quietly. "You've got something to tell me, haven't you?"

"Yes," she began. "It's starts with a mystery, however." She paused and then began again. "Have you noticed how quiet the street has become since Sunday?"

"Quiet? No, what do you mean? It's always quiet here."

"Quiet in an unnatural way — eerie almost. I have the feeling that something happened after we left the anniversary party."

"Haven't noticed anything."

"But I have. Things just aren't right. And I intend to find out what."

"Be careful, Sarah. If it's our neighbors, just don't get involved unless they ask you, and even then..."

"But if it is our friends, we are part of what happened because we were there. I'll find out. People tell me things, you know — sometimes when they don't even mean to."

John looked sadly at her. "Isn't that just the sort of information you don't want to know — gossip?"

"And Celia's car has disappeared," Sarah continued, oblivious to his hesitations. "I always see it parked in their driveway during the day, and now it's missing. There is a strange silence in the street, John, as if everyone was afraid to breathe too deeply. And I haven't seen a soul out."

"It could be your imagination," he offered.

"Yes, of course it could be, and that's why I intend to find out."

~~~

On Thursday morning, early, Sarah drove slowly past the Reilly house on her way to teach a dance class. As she passed by, she caught a glimpse of Jim through the front picture window. For a moment, she had the impression that his face was bandaged. Curious about this impression, she called his real estate office before she returned home and asked to speak with him. But the secretary responded that he had taken the week off and would not be available until the following Monday. Sarah was intrigued — and also worried about spreading gossip — but she assured herself that she could help with what had happened. After all, she had almost a professional, as well as a personal, interest in her friends. And perhaps she could suggest some sort of intervention by the Spiegels. Everyone had met them, and after all, they were experts at resolving marital problems — if the situation demanded it. Yes, she thought with growing decision, she could help if she knew what had happened.

So on the way home in the early afternoon, she stopped in to talk to Christine Barr, hoping that Teddy would still be at the insurance office. When she rang the bell, after parking, she was greeted by Christine, who still wore her blue terry cloth bathrobe. Her hair was frizzled as if she had stopped caring to brush it, and her face was splotched with red welts from rubbing away too many tears.

"Oh, Christine," she exclaimed, pushing her way (uninvited) into the open door. "My God, what's happened? And where is Celia? I haven't seen a trace of her in three days, and then (and here she speculated, hoping to draw out some comment), Jim Reilly injured?"

Christine backed up involuntarily. "You might as well come in," she conceded. "Everyone will know soon enough."

She led Sarah back into the kitchen. Unwashed dishes were stacked on the counter, and a bottle of milk sat open next to cups and saucers still on the breakfast table. There was the faint and unpleasant odor of garbage. Christine turned around and motioned for Sarah to sit down.

"So you know most of the story already, don't you? I didn't think there was any possibility of keeping it a secret. It was so awful; it just had to come out, like a swelling that had to be lanced. And Dan and Jim in a brawl and Jim with a broken nose!"

"How terrible," said Sarah in her most soothing voice, hoping to smooth a passageway of sympathy for more of the story to spill out.

"And now Celia has gone up to Winnetka to stay with her sister!"

"That's a calamity! What in the world happened?"

Christine looked puzzled. "But I thought you knew."

"Yes, of course," Sarah said, recovering her demeanor. "I just don't know all the details, dear. I'm sure if you tell me, you'll feel better."

"Maybe. But nothing actually did happen; that's the sorry and surprising part. That night, after you left the anniversary party, Jim Reilly suggested that we all play a game, and I suppose everyone was so drunk that we just agreed — or at least felt forced to agree. I had no intention of going through with it, but when Celia blew up at Steve and I realized that the men had actually plotted it, I said yes, too, and Jordan and Marie went along. It was a kind of dare, and no one was willing to admit to being the first to call it that. And so, it happened."

"What sort of game?"

"Something one of them got from reading a girlie magazine — the kind that hides under the comic books in the barber shop or under the counter at the Potawatomi newsstand, for all I know. That's where they got the idea."

"And how do you play it?"

"It's like spin the bottle, or maybe Russian roulette — someone said that, actually — but with all the chambers loaded. You pick keys out of a hat, and that's where you end up for the night. My God, I don't know whether I'm more ashamed of myself or just furious at Teddy for going along."

"I think I understand, Christine. But what is so terrible if nothing happened? I take it no one followed through, or did they?

"Well, they say that, but I'll never trust Teddy again. Intention is halfway to doing the deed, isn't it? Maybe worse!"

Sarah paused and then, frowning with concern, put her hand on Christine's shoulder.

"I think I'd like to consult with Candice Overmann about this — perhaps her husband, too," she said resolutely. "And of course, I won't mention names. I'll just say it's something I heard about. I'm sure they'll have some advice. But in the meantime, let me straighten up your kitchen. You go and have a bath. You'll feel better. And I'll see what I can find out. I'll call Candice tonight."

"Well," said Christine, feeling a sense of gratitude that someone had taken control of a situation that had seemed to be growing more fraught with every indecisive moment, "don't bother to put anything away. I'll do that. And thank you, Sarah. You are a friend."

~~~

That afternoon, late, Sarah telephoned Candice Overmann in her office in the psychology department at the University of Chicago. Passed by an officious secretary to her friend, Sarah explained, as best she could, the strange events that had occurred on Golf View Court.

"It's strange, but more than that — intriguing," Candice exclaimed, scarcely trying to disguise the excitement in her voice. "I've heard of such arrangements for wife swapping. The literature on anthropology and psychology is full of descriptions and explanations, and then there are those 19th-century communes in New England and, of course, the Mormons, but I never actually spoke to someone who experienced a sexual potlatch ceremony."

"Is that what it's called?"

"Well, no, not exactly. But that's the idea, isn't it, of exchanging wives as gifts? No, it's my word, but I think it fits. And if there's enough material, perhaps I could write a small commentary somewhere or at least a footnote to the next edition of our book. I'd love to speak to all of the women together, if you could arrange it. I think I could help them to understand, and I'd love to know their reactions," she added.

Sarah paused, wondering whether she was doing the right thing. "But," she began, "I was actually hoping you could give my friends some advice — you know, put it all in context. From what I can tell, they seem to be in a bad way; their marriages seem to be coming unraveled."

"Of course," Candice hastened. "That would be the main idea, to help, and I would only gather material through observation and impression. Of course, if I published anything, I would never use names and places."

"Then I will ask them," replied Sarah. "I suspect they would just like your assurance so they could begin to put their lives back together."

"If you want, then, I could come out on Saturday or Sunday afternoon. I think I'll make this a solo trip. The presence of a man might change the dynamics in a bad way. And, of course, John ought to find something to do away from the house. The appearance of someone from the opposite gender could stifle honesty, and above all, we want an honest accounting."

"If you come on Saturday, he'll be busy at the store. Sunday might be more of a problem. But he'll understand in either case. I'll see what I can arrange."

As soon as Candice hung up, Sarah called Christine and then Marie, both of whom, after some gentle persuasion, agreed to come, and Christine gave her the long-distance number for Celia's sister. But when she talked to Jordan, she was surprised by her angry refusal.

"I'm not speaking to Marie," she said abruptly. "I can't stand to look at her in her flashy clothes and that pretentious two-tone, white-leather Buick convertible, lording it over everyone. No, I won't be coming. And I have nothing to say to your psychologist friend from Chicago. I think she and that partner of hers incited our husbands with all their talk of — what was it? — a complementary marriage."

"Well, perhaps you'll change your mind."

"I doubt it, Sarah. And I think you should mind your own business."

She hung up the phone with a clatter.

Sarah had more luck with Celia, who said she needed to come out to Potawatomi Acres anyway Saturday to pick up more of her things.

"You mean you're staying up there?" ventured Sarah.

"Yes, at least for a while. I've been to see a lawyer already. Things are in motion now, and I guess it would take an effort to halt them. And that's good for me because if it seems to be inevitable, then I won't be so tempted to hesitate and turn back. I want inertia to keep me from changing my mind. Do you understand, Sarah? It's for my own sake that I have to do this. On the other hand, I suppose I could come back to stay in the house, but then Steve would have to move out. Right now, I don't know which is better."

Saturday afternoon was colder and blustery, with a winter wind tearing the leaves and loose branches from trees and sending them in momentary swirls down the street and across the lawns of Golf View Court. Sarah's neighbors arrived punctually at 3 o'clock. Candice had taken the noon train from 59th Street, and Celia had driven. When they were all seated in the living room, Sarah excused herself and returned almost immediately pushing a tea cart, on the top of which were cups and saucers and a large pot inside a quilted cozy. Next to it were a cake with white frosting and a stack of plates and forks.

"I'll serve, if you don't mind," she said, looking around the room at the four women seated in the semicircle of chairs she had arranged. "Tea, everyone?"

"If we're going to talk seriously," said Marie while Sarah was busy cutting the cake, "make mine a scotch. And don't bother about ice."

Sarah complied and then served the others tea and cake. She did so without a word, hoping to make herself a silent observer and no impediment to what Candice had to say.

Everyone looked expectantly at Candice, who pushed back her dark-rimmed glasses with one finger and then pulled her mauve cardigan tighter around her thin chest and began: "I think I know something of what happened here last week," she said, "but perhaps someone could give me the details."

"There aren't any details to give," broke in Marie, "because nothing happened in a happening sense, except that we all saw what our husbands were capable of doing."

"But surely, there are some things that would help me to understand," Candice said hopefully. "I would encourage you to describe how you felt."

"In fact, it's entirely my fault," blurted out Celia as she looked around uncomfortably for a place to settle her plate and cup. "You see, I was so angry and feeling betrayed that Steve could even think of committing adultery on the night of our anniversary party that I just said yes. I never meant it, but I said it anyway, just to hurt him back. I thought it was a horrible, sickening joke and that everyone would just laugh and—"

"It was all our faults," interrupted Christine. "Anyone could have said no. We have that power."

"Yes, you certainly do," chimed in Candice, proudly thinking that Christine was referring to her theory about

"Well, I, for one, didn't feel in control of anything that night," said Marie, "even if nothing happened."

"But something did happen," broke in Celia. "Something terrible happened."

"I know exactly what you mean," replied Candice, "and I wish my husband were here to confirm what I'm going to say, because it's his side of the story, his research that I want to tell you about now."

"Research?!" cried Marie. "How will some academic study help us? What is this, the social science of adultery? Are you going to locate us somewhere on a graph?"

"About men and their needs," continued Candice, ignoring Marie as if she were one of the slower students in her class, "it's really the latest theory, and all of it is in our forthcoming book, but it will help you to understand. I'll try to put it simply:

"You see, as a boy, the male is always competing with his father for the attention of the mother. And the problem is that no one can actually win this struggle. At first, little boys have the impression that they shine brightly in their mother's eyes, and they welcome — in fact, revel in — being touched and cuddled and caressed. That is, until they discover the secret power of the father and his sexual dominance — his hold over the mother and his own prior claim to her intimacy. Recognizing this, the boy begins to feel disgust, both at his own unrequited love — because he feels rejected — and also at the thought of being touched by someone who has been sullied. Most of all, he resents his father for possessing his mother in bed. Strangely, though, he can never lose this sense of competitiveness, and if anything, it becomes stronger. But now it gets redirected to competition with his peers, not for his mother but for any woman. In this way, he is condemned never to win or be entirely satisfied with what can only be a partial victory in possessing a woman — even his wife."

"What the hell does that mean?" interrupted Christine angrily. "Are we supposed to feel sorry for them? Is that what you're saying?"

"Yes, in a way," continued Candice, "because after the terrible shock of recognizing his mother's sexuality, a boy can never thereafter love with complete spontaneity, without the fear of punishment and guilt. In that sense, they never grow up."

"That sounds very strange to me," said Christine again. "I don't think it explains Teddy at all, although I grant you he's still a child. But I just think he was bored and then excited at the thought of getting away with sleeping around and convincing me to approve it."

"Perhaps you don't quite understand yet," smiled Candice, who was thoroughly enjoying the shocked looks of her skeptical audience. "I imagine that the game you played had very strict rules. Am I right?" "Yes," said Celia. "In a way, it did."

"That's the point, then," continued Candice. "You see, in order to break down the normal social taboos — those old taboos that keep us from acting on our most primitive instincts — you have to impose strict new rules to replace them. That's the history of all small societies from the Puritans onward. But in this case, those new rules allowed the men to think they could engage in acts that would have no consequences."

"Do you mean," Marie said with a look of disbelief on her face that melted into a laugh, "do you mean that all this was about getting away with fucking their mothers?"

"Oh, dear," exclaimed Sarah. "I'm sure that's not what she meant."

"But in a way, I do," continued Candice. "You see, if the group rewrites the taboos of society — even if for a short moment — and it substitutes new rules, why, then anything becomes possible. Look at the Mormons and polygamy or the Greeks and the love they encouraged between soldiers and young boys. It's possible, in other words, to redirect and channel our most basic instincts in almost any direction. That's what any society does. And what we think of as normal is simply natural because we have inherited the rules and we don't question them."

Christine interrupted: "Then what you're saying is that morality is just a custom — an outmoded custom?"

"In a sense, yes, a kind of folklore. And that's what all of you experienced that night — a moment of the true suspension of social rules and the temporary invention of new ones. It was a harmless social experiment, and from what you say, no one was hurt by it."

"Well, I was hurt," Celia said, her voice rising. "And I'll never recover from the knowledge of Steve's betrayal, even if I hear some theory that it's a revelation about how society works. Who cares? This was personal! It happened to me! Steve — that's my husband, Mrs. Overmann — was miserable and desperate, which makes him a monster. He gets that way around celebrations. And I think it dawned on him that he was trapped. You see, anniversaries can be dangerous. Either they are routine and regular, like cycles that just pass, or they can break things open and release emotions that can't be tidied up like a messy house. That's my theory! You can have yours!"

"Ah, the death wish," said Candice confidently, "it's in all of us."

"No, you're wrong, at least in Steve's case, and I think I know him well enough," insisted Celia. "He feels that anniversaries are like the jaws of a steel trap, and he wants to free himself and get out while he can. I didn't realize until Friday night how strongly he felt that way. And I certainly didn't believe, until then, that I agreed!"

The room became very silent. All of the women looked at Celia, and Marie finally spoke:

"You amaze me, Celia. I never thought that you could be so blunt. What's happened to you?"

"I was hurt once too often," she replied quietly.

Candice picked up her teacup and sipped the tepid liquid. She began again, not even looking at Celia or acknowledging her outburst.

"I do hope you will, all of you, think about what I've said and try to understand the larger picture, the theory. And please don't do anything rash."

"But we already have," said Marie. "Things have changed. We can't go back to playing bridge every Friday and then dinner at the club on Sunday evening and listening to long, boring stories about errant golf shots. That idyllic life is over and buried. There's your 'death wish' come true!"

"Well, I've done my best," replied Candice.

"Yes, and we thank you," said Sarah. "That was most instructive."

Celia stood and walked to the tea caddy and put her cup and half-eaten cake down.

"I think I'll leave now," she said. "I have a rather long drive."

"Thank you, Sarah," agreed Christine. "I'll be going now, too."

Marie also stood, and all three women picked up their jackets and left abruptly; they had scarcely said goodbye.

When Sarah came back into the living room after seeing them off, Candice was sitting again, looking pensive.

"I'm not sure what good I did. They seem very stubborn and old-fashioned to me," she said. "But perhaps I've learned something myself. Sometimes when your words fall on deaf ears, they come back, as an echo with new meaning. I'll have to think about it, perhaps adjust my theory a bit. And you, Sarah, please write to me in a bit and let me know what happens — the consequences, if there are any. It seems to me that we are in the middle of a process, and who knows where it will go? I'll be fascinated. And," she said, standing and giving over her cup, "please do say hello to John. We must all get together again some time soon."

~~~

That evening, when John returned from the music store, Sarah was sitting in the dark in the living room. Unlike other evenings, there was no odor of spices or of any cooking in the air, and it was obvious that she had not begun to fix dinner.

"I think I've made a terrible mistake," she began when he came in and sat beside her, "inviting Candice out to talk to the wives on the street. She seemed to make them angrier by talking about abstract psychology. I'm afraid of the consequences of what she said, although I imagine she believes that she has come across fascinating material for her next article. But people aren't footnotes, John. Sometimes I just forget to be friends and think sympathetically. They thought she was trying to justify what the men planned."

"You tried to help," said John. "That's all we can do. But remember, I did warn you."

"Yes, you did. And I'm not pleased with what Candice said. Not pleased at all. I think Jordan was right to see it would be trouble."

"Didn't she come then?" asked John.

"No, and she seemed pretty angry."

~~~

Although several of the wives and husbands on Golf View Court were fearful that the whole town would quickly learn about the key party, the waves of rumor lapped closest to home at first. Fortunately, Dan Clements' law partners remained ignorant of the key party. But somehow Edgar and Dan Jr. found out some of the details of their parents' escapades that night, and

Marie, when she learned of this, began to interpret every act of the boys as an overt rebellion against her and Dan, a retribution for their transgressions. It became impossible for her to separate the mild seductions of juvenile delinquency — something everyone was talking about in magazines and on the radio — from the anger and shame and embarrassment that she sometimes believed to motivate their behavior. Not only did their demeanor become more deeply sullen but their childhood seemed to have reached an abrupt end. More than once, Dan said that his behavior that night had become an excuse for their misbehavior and a justification for their testing the limits of any rules that he tried to impose. In a kind of horrible travesty of the old adage "like father, like son," both boys had shown a streak of willfulness, and more than once, he believed that they were on the verge of saying that if he could act like an outlaw, then they could, too.

There was another person in town who knew the details of the wife swapping party, Reverend White at the Potawatomi Community Church. He had only learned about it because Marie had visited him one afternoon to confess her troubles with her sons and to ask for advice.

Marie had driven to the church to consult Reverend White on a chilly day in November, about a month after the party. She was not a particularly devout Christian or even a regular attendee at church, although she and Dan placed themselves high on the donors list every year and she sometimes went to services (without Dan). In fact, she had not been sure why she wanted the reverend's advice, except that she had believed he might find some way to intervene with the boys. Aside from teachers, he was the one adult who knew them best because they had both been, if briefly, Boy Scouts and he had often helped the scoutmaster and even substituted at meetings when the scoutmaster was out of town. This scouting interest related primarily to Reverend White's one hobby, aside from nurturing his flock. He had a collection of Indian artifacts, and in Indian lore he was somewhat of a minor expert. In his spare time, he had learned something of the Potawatomi tribe, which had once inhabited the area, and he had a small collection of arrowheads and stone axes that had surfaced in various construction sites around town. Some of them, it was said, derived from the desperate battle at Starved Rock, on the Illinois River west of town. Most citizens and members of the church knew of his interest, and they contributed to his hobby. He, in turn, often brought specimens to Scouting events.

On this particular day, Marie had, as usual, paid special attention to her dress, choosing a dark business suit and a white ruffled blouse. The only adornment of the coat was a large silver brooch, which she wore over her left breast. She wanted to give the impression of serious intent yet elicit what she believed was her proper due — respect and admiration.

The church, which she entered that afternoon, smelled of scorched paint, oil and damp rugs, evidence that the heat had just been turned on and the building was burning off its accumulated smells from the warm summer and fall. The lights in the narthex were dim, but one lone bright spot shone near the altar and the choir stalls. Marie heard the organ playing, and one particular passage — no doubt difficult — was repeated three or four times. She paced up the central aisle and then turned left, under the perched pulpit from which Reverend White preached every Sunday, to the hallway that led to the church offices. She had been in this area of the building several times but had always found the contrast striking, between the solemn, heavy atmosphere of the place of worship and the sparsely decorated and severe appointments of the business wing. Only Reverend White's private office echoed the elaborate and expensive taste of the church that most worshippers experienced.

Knocking on the door — punctual for her appointment, made by telephone with his secretary — Marie heard a hearty invitation to enter. Reverend White was sitting behind his very large carved desk of mahogany, relaxing in a swivel chair. One of the two objects on the desk was a large writing work pad with leather edges and a removable green piece of blotting paper. No doubt, she thought as she entered, this was where he wrote his sermons. There was also a framed photograph of his family turned outward so that anyone sitting in front of the desk could study and admire it. There were five smiling faces — with the reverend in civilian clothes, his arm around his diminutive wife, and their three children arranged in stepladder fashion on the other side. It struck her as curious that the picture faced whoever sat in front of him, as if he were conveying the reassuring message that he, too, was a member of the community, a man of

God but of prudent and circumspect faith and not given over to excesses of spirituality — a family man.

Today the reverend was in half-mufti. He was wearing his typical black shirt, but it lacked its stiff white collar. Marie could see, hanging on a clothes tree beside the desk, a black robe with velvet cross bands on the sleeves and, next to it, a dark sports coat. He rose to welcome her.

"Mrs. Clements," he began. "I'm delighted to see you. My secretary has informed me that you wish some sort of consultation. And of course, that's exactly why I'm here, to be at your service."

Marie was slightly amused at his formality, but she was also serious and worried and wanted his advice.

"It's my boys; I think you know them," she began, at the periphery of her problem. "They seem to have gone haywire suddenly. They are full of mischief. No, that's not the right word. I mean anger and misbehavior. Dan and I really don't know what to do. It's as if they blame us for something terrible."

"Yes, I know Dan Jr. and Edmund pretty well."

"Edgar."

"Well, in my experience, Marie — if I may — the young go through turbulent times at the end of adolescence. That's about their age, as I remember. All the best sociology and psychology confirms that. It's just part of growing up — resentful of parents, rebellious behavior. Of course, I don't know your special circumstances, but perhaps it's only that."

"I thought so at first myself," resumed Marie. "But it is so obviously something else because it's such a sudden onset."

"And do you know what that might be?"

Marie hesitated. She had come to see Reverend White specifically to tell him about what had transpired at the anniversary party, but once in his presence, she wondered whether this was a wise decision.

"Are you sworn to secrecy?" she began. "I've heard that in the Catholic confession, the priest never reveals what a parishioner confides in him — the sins of confession, that is."

"My dear Mrs. Clements — Marie — I'm sure we don't have to be Catholics to trust one another, do we? Everything about my position depends upon the faith that you put in me. I would never compromise that. And I can't advise you unless you tell me what you think might be the root of your problem."

Marie hesitated again, but then she began a very brief description of the key party. As she did so, she felt acutely embarrassed, especially as she noticed that Reverend White was looking away when she described what had happened. "Perhaps," she thought, "he is trying to hide any emotions he might have — and his disapproval of me."

When she had finished, he looked intently at her and said: "What a terrible story; such a betrayal of marriage. I'm simply amazed; you are all such fine citizens and members of the church and the country club. You are people who matter in this community."

"I'm sorry, Reverend, but I have come to terms with it. It's not my purpose to ask forgiveness or clear myself of sin. I'm most worried about my sons."

"Do you think they have found out what happened?"

"Yes, I fear exactly that. In fact, I'm sure of it. Not everything, of course, but Edgar did see Dan and Jim Reilly fighting, and somehow he and Dan Jr. found out more of the details. And now I think they are misbehaving as a way of testing us or, worse, getting back at us somehow, punishing us."

"That seems to me to be very plausible," said Reverend White in his most authoritative voice.

"But then, what should we do? I mean, what should I do — because Dan doesn't even know that I've come to see you, and he wouldn't approve."

"Wouldn't approve? But why not? Surely, you only want advice."

"He's terrified that his law partners will find out, for one. And to be frank, he doesn't have much faith in the church, any church. He's the sort that always tries to find his own way."

"In some respects, Marie, that's a very admirable trait. But it sounds to me as if he lost his way, if only temporarily. Certainly, you can trust me not to gossip. What you did is, after all, between you and God, and I know that your coming here today is a way of opening up communication with him, through me. It's the right thing to do."

"Do you really think so?"

"Oh, yes. And the best advice I can give you is to open your heart and admit what happened to him. That's the best way to heal yourself. And you can't help your boys if you hide what you did from God."

"Perhaps," said Marie, "but I really don't feel guilty, because I didn't do anything, not really. After all, it was only a game."

"Well, that's not entirely the point, is it? Don't we live in a time when we have learned that what people think and what they say is almost more dangerous than what they dare to do? I'm sure you know what I mean. The world is a perilous place — even here in Potawatomi Acres. Immorality can be a kind of infection, polluting the whole community. And just because what you did had some sort of invented rules, how does that make it right?"

He continued: "And as for a remedy, I would advise you to never talk to your boys about this. Whatever they know should just be buried. Time will heal them. There is so much else that is happening in their young, changing lives, and a graphic description of that party would surely destroy their faith in you completely. You do see that, don't you? Only God can forgive you, not your children and surely not me."

"Perhaps I understand," said Marie, frowning. "And you won't say anything?" She paused and then stood up abruptly. "Thank you so much for your time, Reverend. You are a comfort."

She knew that she had replied a bit hastily, but she suddenly had the feeling that her confession had been a mistake, and she wanted nothing more than to leave. She stood and shook his outstretched hand.

"Anytime, Marie," he said, lowering the tone of his voice by a half-octave, to a pitch he imagined was reassuring.

She turned and walked quickly out of the office and back through the church. The organist had moved on to another passage and pulled out different stops, producing a voice of gurgles and murmurs that followed her out like pursuing rumors. Marie hastened through the front door and to the Buick parked in the small side lot, not realizing that Reverend White was watching through the leaded glass windows of the rectory. She feared now that she would regret her decision to confide in him. He had been no help at all — the opposite, in fact. She was now more worried than ever. She would have to live with it, yes, but she had expected something more, some suggestion about how to communicate better with her sons. But he had only advised evasion and secrecy, and that, she understood, was the source of the problem. And really, what help would prayer be? Well, she would heed his advice about Edgar and Dan Jr., but she thought a good deal less of him for giving it.

She glanced back as she reached her car and saw a faint shadow in the rectory window, blurred by the thick panes. Presumably, it was Reverend White, she thought, watching her. Just as suddenly, he was gone. Perhaps, she supposed, it had been her imagination. And it was just as well that she did not see him pick up the telephone and ask the operator to ring his house. When his wife answered, he merely said — answering her surprise at his willingness to interrupt his day — "I wanted to warn you about something rather terrible. You may hear about it from someone else. But do ignore anything, and let me explain when I get home. Goodbye, dear," he said without waiting for a response, and then he hung up.

He looked out the window again and saw that Marie's Buick had left the lot.

~~~

The next morning, Sarah sat in her kitchen, drinking a cup of black coffee and absently contemplating the early frost that lay across the back lawn, light as a spun web. Beads of water glistened on the tallest blades of grass and dripped from the trees and bushes. It occurred to her suddenly that if she walked outside, across this blanket of hoar, her shoes would leave imprints on the still green grass beneath. Although she could not see it, she imagined that the golf course beyond the trees was also covered by thick frost. It would, of course, burn off quickly, with the clear day's sun. But this lacy harbinger of winter cheered her with thoughts of a rousing fire in the living room and long weekend afternoons when the slanting sun would fill the room and warm her back as she read or chatted with John. Yet she was faintly uneasy, as if some dark cloud threatened to blow a shadow across the scene before her. Looking at the almost bare maple tree, its dark branches like insect appendages directly in front of her, she imagined for a moment a black spider waiting patiently, observing and preparing to strike. And then she shook this bleak thought off and wondered for a moment at her ability to imagine such a voiceless rumor of calamity.

She stirred slightly as she heard a distant door close. John was up, probably making his way to the bathroom, and in a minute, he would join her. And then her early morning solitude would be broken up into practical tasks, preparing for the day ahead. Nonetheless, she sat for one more delicious moment and imagined the backyard again, now as a friendlier scene. She thought of the almost erotic feeling of the wet, cold grass on her bare feet were she to slip out the back door for a moment and dance on the unbroken gossamer stage. But John would never approve; he always set limits.

"Right," she said out loud. She stood to stretch in a slow, lazy pirouette. Just as she balanced back on her heels, the telephone began to ring, with a sharp, distressing tone. John had turned up the sound on the two extensions in the house because of the loud music he played and her fear of missing a call. Nonetheless, hearing its piercing one this early puzzled her. She walked to the black phone attached to the wall next to the door. Almost unconsciously, she glanced at the large clock over the refrigerator. It indicated 8:15.

She grasped the receiver in her hand and then sat down on the stool next to the small, elevated writing table.

"Hello, Vollmer residence," she said, almost as if she were asking a question.

"Oh, it's you, Sarah."

"Yes." She paused, not quite recognizing the voice for an instant.

"It's Jordan, Jordan Reilly. I'm awfully sorry to bother you this morning, and so early. But I thought you might be off teaching today and gone before I could reach you."

"No, I'm not due until much later today."

"Good then." There was a long pause, and then Jordan began again, this time with no apology and all the warmth of her voice dissipated and replaced by an accusatory tone.

"I'm very distressed."

"Yes," Sarah replied quickly.

"Well, you're the only person who knew, so it has to be you."

"I'm sorry," replied Sarah, "but I'm confused, Jordan." She allowed her voice to fall into a similarly hostile register. "I'm not sure what I know or what the problem is."

"The problem is malicious gossip!" Jordan replied quickly. "I heard late last night. Don't ask me who told me, but someone has been spreading rumors about — you know, about the anniversary party and that awful game. And you're the only one who knows besides that dreadful friend of yours from Chicago. And now, it seems, there are other people. And you're the only one who could have... We trusted you, Sarah, and now..."

Sarah allowed a long moment of silence to pass because she feared that a quick answer would seem glib and insincere.

"How terrible," she finally said. "That's simply awful. And they didn't say how they found out?"

"Then you didn't talk to anyone?"

"No, of course not. Only you and Christine and Celia and, of course, Marie. And Overmann. But she doesn't know anyone else in Potawatomi Acres. I'm sure of that. And I would never, never."

"But how well do you know this Chicago person? She must have talked after that meeting at your house."

"Jordan," interrupted Sarah, "you weren't even here. How can you presume?"

"And now you know why I wouldn't join your little confession and therapy session. This is exactly what I feared all along."

"That's very unfair, Jordan. Overmann would never say anything. She's a scientist, not a gossip."

There was a long pause, and Jordan began again, almost discouraged. "Well, perhaps you're right. But someone did talk, and the story I had last night was a good deal more lurid and detailed than anything that actually occurred."

"I'm terribly sorry, Jordan, but I'm certain you are wrong."

"I suppose I believe you, Sarah. I just had to make sure. I mean, there's a certain solidarity among us on Golf View Court, isn't there? In spite of what happened, we're almost our own community, aren't we?"

"Yes," said Sarah. "Yes." She repeated herself to be persuasive.

"Well, please don't say a word to anyone. People can exaggerate so terribly."

"But as you all said, nothing happened. Just a game. Just words."

"That's not the point."

"No, I imagine not."

"Well, goodbye, Sarah," Jordan said. "And thank you. So sorry to call so early, but..." She hung up. Sarah held the receiver for a moment longer before she replaced it slowly.

"Did I hear voices and the telephone?" asked John, appearing in the doorframe. He had dressed for work in gray flannel slacks and a brown sports coat. Sarah noticed that he was wearing a red tartan sweater vest, the first time he had put it on this season.

"Yes, Jordan Reilly called. I'm afraid that the story of the anniversary party is out and making the rounds of gossip. She got a call from someone but wouldn't say who. It's just as I feared. And she thought I had started the rumors. I don't know about our friends, John — if they still are our friends. How could she think that? And she didn't sound convinced at all. She'll think that I'm even guiltier than she is, than they are. How does the telling suddenly become worse than the act?"

"But you didn't say anything?" John asked.

"Of course not. Of course not. I didn't even want to know. How could you doubt me?"

"I'm sorry. I know you didn't. But rumors — they're like fading musical chords. You know, when a piece ends, the sound continues in the air for a moment, and you can still hear it — feel it — even when it's gone."

"That's a pretty thought, John, I'll grant you, but you're wrong. Someone talked, and now they will all fight like cats in a bag."

"Nice metaphor," John laughed. "So is this another chapter for your analysis then?"

"Yes, I hadn't thought of it, but you're right. And I suppose that any good anthropologist would understand that recounting an event always has more consequences than its doing. That's why memory and tradition linger. But I don't want any part of this story anymore."

~~~

Jordan replaced the receiver on the cradle of the telephone that sat on the hall table and walked back into the kitchen. The situation, she understood, was bleak — even desperate. The snitch — that's what she'd love to call the guilty person who had revealed the story to his or her face — had let loose something uncontrollable. She knew that denying it would only increase its aura of truth and that finding out who was responsible would do nothing to diminish its force. Still, she wanted to know; she felt she had to know. That was why she had accused Sarah first, because she did not want it to be one of her closest friends. But now the circle of guilt had tightened.

"Jim," she called suddenly. "Come down here immediately. I have to talk to you."

She heard a muffled reply from upstairs and then the clumsy, heavy tread of her husband clumping down the stairs. She walked into the kitchen to wait for him. When he appeared, she saw with distaste that he was dressed only in his brown slacks and an off-white sleeveless undershirt. His hairy arms and shoulders almost made her shudder with disgust.

"You took your time," she said. "I wouldn't have called you unless it mattered."

"Well, I'm here," he replied peevishly. "I'm not the dog; fetch, fetch! What's the problem?"

"Very funny," she replied, trying to remain calm. "I've just been on the phone with Sarah Vollmer. I thought that she might have been the one. But now I'm not sure. At least I had hoped it was her."

"Her?" said Jim. "I need a clue, Jordan. Why not tell me what you're talking about?"

"The story of the party is out. Someone called me last night to ask if it was true. How could they know unless someone talked? There were too many details — even about you and your fight with Dan."

"But nothing happened, so who cares?"

"You ought to, you fool. Don't you think your real estate business will cave in like some shoddy hut if you lose respectability? Who would buy a house from someone who tries to sleep with every woman in the neighborhood?"

"But I didn't."

"Yes, indeed, you didn't because someone punched you before you could. But you would have. You're a fool and a coward, too!"

"That's unfair, completely unfair."

"Since when is gossip fair? Do you think that anyone hearing a juicy story ever tries to find the truth? What world do you live in, Jim?"

"Well," he replied slowly, "you may be right. I hadn't thought about the business."

"And I have to do that for you, too," replied Jordan angrily. "You and your damned original idea and your stupid, stupid friends. Do you think one of them talked? It's not inconceivable."

"No, honestly, Jordan, I can't see that. Men aren't like that."

"Aren't like what?"

"Well, I can't see Dan or Steve or Teddy bragging about how they didn't have the guts to go through with it. Not their style."

"Oh, then I'm completely convinced," she said sarcastically. "If you had managed to pull it off, if Dan hadn't broken your nose, then you would have shouted it from the rooftops: 'Look at me! I fucked Marie Clements!'"

"Don't be vulgar, Jordan. No call for it."

"Vulgar?!" she shouted. "You're the one who's vulgar! Now get out of my kitchen. And put on a shirt. I can't bear the sight of you; you're disgusting."

Jordan turned away before he could respond and walked slowly to the stove to put on water for coffee. Jim would get instant this morning, and he could eat whatever he liked, as long as she didn't have to prepare it. As for herself, she had no appetite at all. Today she would only feed the dog and then be done with it.

As she ran the water into the kettle, she thought about calling some of the others, but she realized she had no intention of communicating with Marie; they were hardly speaking. And Celia or Christine, she couldn't bear the thought of accusing them and then listening to their shocked and dishonest denials. What was the point? The story was out. So be it. She was almost eager to embrace the consequences. It was like waiting for some fatal diagnosis or maybe the promise of a gradual remission. In any case, nothing could be done, and there was something immensely satisfying and exciting, almost erotic, about that.

When the water boiled, she took a tea bag from a plastic canister on the shelf beside the stove, balanced it — tag hanging outside — in her favorite porcelain mug, embossed with black Scotties jumping and cavorting, and poured the hot liquid inside. She impatiently dunked the bag repeatedly, spilling and splashing water over the top. Finally, when it was dark enough, she walked to the refrigerator, pulled out an open carton of cream and poured it in, watching the heavy swirl disappearing and then ascending again to lighten the brew. Ordinarily, this reaction would have pleased her immensely. She loved moments by herself when she could anticipate the coming day. But this morning, the period ahead seemed to be without promise. Of course, she would feel better once Jim had left and she could sit quietly and try to evaluate what had happened and what the consequences would be. Even without seriously considering it, she knew that all the ties that had bound the residents of Golf View together had snapped like a cheap rubber band. In a way, she didn't really care because an end to cloying friendships could be liberating — like an amicable divorce. If she and Jim had to move away, so be it. There was nothing to hold them here. They could move on —

whether they stayed together or not; and she really didn't care about that, either.

It was remarkable, she thought, how quickly friendships could turn to suspicion and anger — if it really was friendship and not just some sort of convenience that had thrown them all together. She wondered now whether she had ever actually liked Celia or Christine. They were so common and boring, with their petty complaints and jealousies; she realized that she had long hated such weaknesses. And the events of the past few hours convinced her that she had always detested Marie, with her fancy car, her clothes and her fabricated sophistication. As Jordan picked up her cup to go into the living room, she heard Jim trudging down the steps.

"Bye," he called in a voice that already had the tone of an earnest Realtor. "I'll get a coffee and roll in the village. And the mail's here. See you later."

Jordan walked to the front hall and picked up the letters and bills. Just as quickly, she tossed them down on the table and glanced at the magazine that had arrived in a brown sleeve. She ripped it open and pulled out the latest issue of Life. The black-and-white cover featured the photo of a ship on stilts, something about a hydrofoil, and a lead story about the New York Yankees. She quickly looked inside for anything interesting to read while she finished her tea and saw, toward the end of the table of contents, an article titled "Life Plays a New Party Game." She threw it down, half in disgust and half in amusement, knowing full well that it would never be something about wife swapping. Never in Life! "How ironic," she said. But it made her think as she walked into the living room about games — not just the key party but the games they were all playing. She sat down on the couch, and Sammy, who had been following her closely, bounded over to beg for attention.

"Not now, Sammy dear," she exclaimed, pushing his paws off her lap. "Later. I want to think seriously for a moment."

As she sipped the dregs of her tea, she almost said out loud: "Games!" And almost simultaneously, as she thought the word, it came to her that they had all been playing games; they had made life into a game, a sport and an amusement like the innocent magazine title. They acted as if nothing was real, she thought, unless it could be played — golf, bridge, marriage, divorce, selling real estate, sex even. Sex especially! Everything had rules to be followed, and nothing could be spontaneous. That was why she could not think of her life with Jim as in any way separate from the golf course or the rounds of bridge on Fridays and the tedious repetition of cocktail parties. There was nothing that seemed genuine in their lives unless it could conform to made-up instructions and guidelines. And now it was all collapsing because they had tried to play a game that cheated on all the other rules of their lives. But was that the problem, or did they feel empty and angry because nothing happened? Well, she thought, something did happen because there were real consequences. She felt both excited and apprehensive about not knowing the future.

~~~

On Saturday afternoon, Marie dressed in the smart light-brown tailored wool suit she had recently purchased, spending several minutes deciding whether to wear a silk scarf of red and purple flames tucked into the top of her white blouse. At last, she selected it. Looking at the neat shoe rack, with its four rows of pairs, she chose light-brown Mary Jane pumps with open toes. She would be overdressed, but she felt the need for it. Due at a committee meeting at the club to plan the winter dinner-dance, she understood that her presence had nothing to do with golf or sport; her only reason for being there was to ensure that elegance prevailed at this dead-season social.

After she handed the Buick over to the eager valet standing at the portico by the front entrance, she climbed the steps and entered the reception area. To the right was a wing containing several smaller offices and meeting rooms, and to the left, the cocktail bar, offering gloomy hospitality before the evening pre-dinner rush. She noticed the unpleasant odor of the locker room; the smell of damp and musty clothes leaked all the way there, and she thought, momentarily, to say something about it to the manager. When she glanced into the half-lit bar, she could make out only two figures, a man and a woman having cocktails in the corner, almost out of sight. For no reason except curiosity, she edged closer and immediately recognized Mrs. Smith sitting with Teddy Barr. She stopped immediately, almost catching her heel on the rug. As she faltered, Mrs. Smith looked up and stared at her, and then Mrs. Smith suddenly broke into a broad grin. She raised her glass and tipped it in a mock salutation and then looked away. If Teddy caught any of this silent communication, he did not turn to acknowledge it or wonder about its intention. In fact, Marie thought, he dropped his shoulders as if to hide his presence.

"So," Marie said to herself, "that's her game."

As Marie walked down the corridor to her committee meeting, Mrs. Smith gestured with her martini glass toward the departing figure and said to Teddy, "There goes Marie Clements. Busy, busy, isn't she? Always the official. Or should I say officious?"

Teddy turned around and glanced uncomfortably in her direction. "Marie likes to be the center of things."

"And you, too, Teddy, you're content just as you are?"

"Well, yes, of course. Why shouldn't I be? A man my age, in good health except for my bum leg, and a long marriage. Daughter in college. Career swimming along nicely."

"Sounds dreadful to me," exclaimed Mrs. Smith. Then she leaned closer to the table. "I suppose that's why you wanted a little excitement the other night. A taste of sophistication."

"I guess you know the details then. Everyone else seems to."

"Of course I do. Not that I care much. You can't imagine how many friends called to tell me."

"Then you know that nothing happened, don't you? Some of the guys got cold feet and backed out."

Mrs. Smith just smiled and took a sip of her drink, dabbing her bright red lips with a napkin when she put her glass down.

"That includes you, too, I suppose. So now what?" she asked.

"I don't know, Agnes," said Teddy, lowering his voice. "We'll get through it, I suppose. And then back to normal."

"And that is?"

"Just more of the same, I guess." Teddy looked at her carefully. He could see the shallow ridges of her deeply tanned face under her heavy makeup. Of course, he thought, she's a bottle blonde — and not quite so young as she appeared from a distance. But there was still something immensely attractive about her — a gracefulness and a warmth that he found in few other women. Divorce had given her power and attraction and availability; it seemed to free her. And she seemed to be interested in him. Wasn't that first base?

"But what about you, Agnes? I've always wondered why you stayed here in Potawatomi Acres. You could have gone anywhere, right?"

"Just the house and the club, I suppose, and my friends."

"I hope you count me as one of them?"

"I suppose I do, Teddy, of course!"

"I was hoping to be more like a special friend." Teddy mumbled, less sure of himself and hesitating as he chose his words. "Someone you can rely on, someone—"

"Well, I'm not unaware of what your wife thinks of me — in fact, what all the wives in the Golf View Quartet think of me. It's not so easy, you know, to be a single woman."

"But you're not single; you're divorced," Teddy interrupted.

"Now that's just what I mean. It's like I have a scarlet letter pinned to my breast — a bright red D for divorce. Or is it dalliance? I can't see it, but it seems all you lot can. Why do you think I play that charade with all of you?"

Teddy was dismayed. This was not the direction he had hoped the conversation would take. He had hoped for tender words, not this sudden revelation of bitterness.

"I'm sorry, Agnes. I don't know what to say. I certainly don't feel that way about you. Not me!"

"Yes, you do, Teddy, especially you!" she exclaimed. "That's exactly how you feel! You think I'm defenseless and that I'll sleep with you because when the law separated me from Frank, I somehow lost all my morals. Poor old Frank! At least he had the sense to leave me with some money. But he was such a loser. But no, I don't think I will. You're still an attractive man, Teddy, with a few inches of tread left on your tires. But I don't think I will. So let's just be friends. I'd like to keep it like that."

Teddy was silent for a moment as he felt a flush of embarrassment spreading over his face. He grabbed his drink and took a healthy swig and then set it down abruptly.

"I do suppose I ought to go home. Christine, you know," he said, awkwardly rising and bumping the table so that it jostled and spilled her drink. "I guess so," he said, pushing back resolutely and turning away. His stiff leg made him hobble for a moment, as if his injury had just recurred.

"Yes," she called after him.

~~~

Marie had turned to cross the hallway again and entered the wing where the meeting room was located. When she stepped inside the wood-paneled room, with its shelves of golf trophies and photos of smiling players, she could see that most of the members had already assembled. There were six women — including the dowdy wife of the club manager, whom she detested, his secretary and three others like Marie, the wives of prominent members — who constituted the social committee. She nodded to everyone and took a seat at the large oblong table. The head chair, the manager's place, was still empty. The group remained silent, but the residue of an animated discussion still hung in the room like a fading memory. But no one spoke, and even if all of them looked at her long enough to appraise her suit, their glances measured none of the effusive admiration that her clothes usually inspired. She could sense that their looks were scornful, perhaps even jealous, as if she had dressed to embarrass them, which, of course, she had.

When Ed Thornton appeared and settled into his manager's seat, he looked around the room casually until he saw Marie. He paused and then pursed his lips as if to say something, but he just nodded and then moved on to recognize all the others by name. Marie only half listened to his droning list of projects. He discussed the usual dance band, which she remembered could only play slow-motion versions of current hits and a few old-time melodies from the 1930s and '40s, and their pasty-faced has-been jazz singer, whose exaggerated gestures wiggled in the air like the vibrato she lacked. She thought, for a moment, to suggest a band that didn't wear white dinner jackets and white buck shoes and could play the sort of music her sons listed to on their record player. But when she raised her hand, tentatively, the manager simply ignored her, although his wife scowled at her and flushed a blotchy red color, visible through her unevenly smeared makeup. Nonetheless, she had a sly look of triumph on her face. Marie almost felt sorry for her despite the snub.

The most important decision, as always, was the choice of a theme, because it determined the food and the decorations. Last year had been Hawaiian, and Marie hoped for something more inventive than pineapple drinks, gaudy shirts, ukulele music and flower leis.

"Perhaps we could do Paris," she blurted out, not waiting for the manager to recognize her. "I'm sure everyone has seen the movie with Gene Kelly and Leslie Caron, and there are so many wonderful songs about the city, as well as the obvious food and decor. It's a natural choice," she continued. "I'm sure the members would be delighted."

There was a long moment of silence, interrupted finally by Mrs. Appleby, wife of the local dentist.

"I prefer something a little less risque," she said, stopping on the last word so as to demonstrate her passing acquaintance with high-school French. "Oh, I know that some people think about Paris as romantic. But isn't it really just a giant brothel over there? I mean, you know, the demimonde of nightclubs and cabarets and that awful cancan dance. Of course, Marie, perhaps it's a seductive atmosphere you're after." She concluded with a defiant smirk that brought a renewed flush of red to the face of the manager's wife.

"Are there other suggestions?" asked the manager.

"An English country estate," replied Mrs. Appleby enthusiastically. "What with the coronation of the queen last year, everyone has been talking about England. It could be so elegant. Perhaps we could make it a costumed ball."

Marie thought maliciously but held back from remarking that the club's menu of burnt steaks, overcooked vegetables, roast beef and gluey puddings was certainly within the ability of the chef and that he could appropriately call it English fare and not change a thing — and not insult the words "English cuisine."

"Entirely suitable," said the manager quickly. "Now, if we could have a vote?"

Everyone in the room, except Marie, raised her hand. Instead, she stood abruptly.

"I've another appointment," she said curtly. "If you want me to work on anything, just let me know."

"Of course, Mrs. Clements, of course. We will call on you should you be needed," replied the manager as she opened the door and quickly walked out and down the hall toward the reception area. She stopped for a moment and took a deep breath to control her anger. It was clear that they knew and this was the beginning of her punishment and isolation. Looking vaguely across the room, she could see that the bar was still only half-illuminated, but now it was empty. When she had parked the Buick in the driveway, she made her way slowly into the house. The boys, she knew, would be out with friends, and Dan was probably watching a golf match on television. She suddenly felt immensely weary and depressed, as if the life that stretched before her were something she had already experienced, as if she were walking backward and contemplating a future she knew too well as the past, where every petty rise and depression in her path already bore her footprints. She could predict the vapid small talk and silences of Dan and the indifference and hostility of her children for as long as they remained at home. And then when they were off to college, she would be alone with Dan again. Even her extravagance had brought no more than a brief reproach from him; clearly, that was no way to make him pay for her unhappiness. Nothing seemed to stir him from his self-satisfaction. And now there was the judgment of the community to face. The faces that once admired her had turned smug and disapproving. As she entered the kitchen, she glared at the unwashed dishes in the sink. But when her eyes lit on the telephone, she suddenly had an idea that gave her a malicious delight. She cleared her throat and picked up the receiver, almost giddy with pleasure. Clicking the contact three times, she said to the operator:

"Please get me Christine Barr."

Teddy answered, and Marie regretted for a moment that she could not see his face when she asked for Christine.

"Yes, Marie?"

"Hello, Christine. I'm sorry to bother you."

"Yes?"

"But I was just at the club — at the dinner-dance committee meeting — and I saw something disturbing."

"About the committee? Don't tell me that Ida Appleby was up to her usual."

"Yes, she was, but no, not that. It's about Mrs. Smith, whom you and Celia have been going on about. I don't really know how to tell you this gently, so I'll be blunt. She was having cocktails with Teddy. I only saw him from the back, but I'm sure."

"Well, you are always blunt, Marie!" exclaimed Christine. "And I suppose you just couldn't wait to get home to tell me! Thanks for the scouting report!" She slammed down the phone.

Marie heard the connection break as if an overhead wire had snapped. She smiled as she gently replaced the receiver.

"Who was that?" asked Dan as he strode into the room.

"Nobody. Christine," Marie replied without looking at him.

"Did she confess to spreading the story?"

"No, she didn't. And anyway, I'm sure I know now, so I'd better tell you. It was me, or rather, Reverend Whitehead. I went to ask him for advice about the boys, and I suppose I told him everything about the anniversary party. He swore he wouldn't talk, but I imagine he told his wife — and she doesn't abide by any vows. I'm sorry, Dan, but it would have gotten out anyway."

Dan studied her back and then grabbed her by the shoulders and turned her around.

"Just for once," he shouted, "just for once, stop hiding behind all your fancy clothes, your justifications, and talk to me like a human being! Come out into the open, because this is serious. I don't care who talked here. It's much worse than that. I suppose you know that Celia has hired a member of my firm to represent her in her divorce. And of course, your friend, you dear bridge partner, has obviously told him everything. So it's not just the damned community here that knows, but soon my partners will be laughing behind my back. And do you know that the one thing that can get me expelled from the firm is what they call "moral turpitude"? Dishonesty, taking a bribe — anything else would just get your hand slapped, because you can talk your way out of it. Even a blatant affair with one of the secretaries would pass. But a public humiliation is like a trial, conviction and sentence all in one, with everyone the judge, jury and curious public!"

Marie looked at him, wondering whether her loathing for him reflected on her face, and then she broke free of his grip. She had almost unconsciously shuddered at his threat and the possibility of disgrace, but worse was the likelihood of some change in their status. She wouldn't care at all about his career if not for the fact that she and her sons depended on him. But there was nothing she could do now, except perhaps confront Reverend Whitehead. It would not undo the damage, but it would give her some satisfaction if she could make him squirm.

~~~

On Sunday morning, Marie dressed with her usual care but picked out a modest dark green wool suit, with a pale, lime-colored blouse and a simple strand of cultured pearls. She chose her ordinary black pumps. The only gesture to style was her black alligator handbag with the brass edging and eyeball snaps. She wore just enough makeup to suggest an effort but nothing to seem extravagant.

Neither of the boys was up yet, and if Dan was curious about her destination, he said nothing as she prepared to leave. Without asking, she took the keys to the Buick and roared the engine when she started it up. Whether she planned it or not, she ground the gears putting it into first after backing out of the driveway.

The trip was not long, merely across town to the location of the church, which sat next to the schoolyard and about four blocks behind the train station. As she drove, she was reminded of the small circumference of the village, its constrained dimensions and, she thought bitterly, its narrow-mindedness. Even if Dan's practice survived, she planned to insist on leaving this place forever. She had no hope of repairing her marriage, but perhaps a new environment would allow them both to lead a more or less separate life together. Until the boys were gone, divorce was out of the question. But perhaps then. At least that was something to anticipate and imagine, and above all, she wanted to be able to think about some sort of future that didn't involve this one-stoplight town.

After she parked the car in the large lot behind the church, she walked toward the front door. Next to the entrance, there was a large aluminum case with a glass front and black backing behind the words of the day's sermon: "What God Knows." She walked into the darkened church, under the western rose window, which she and Dan had helped to finance, and up the rug that divided the rows of smooth wooden pews, with their shelves of black hymnals. The organist was playing something indistinct, perhaps something improvised to sound like an introit. She sat down toward the center. The room was fairly crowded, and she recognized a number of acquaintances — parents of children her boys knew and friends from the club. But no one spoke to her or even looked in her direction, and she remained alone in her pew. She crossed her legs and leaned back after picking the hymnal from its perch. She saw that the processional would be "Cleanse Me." She turned to the page and read without trying to pick out the melody:

Search me, O God,
And know my heart today.
Try me, O Savior,
Know my thoughts, I pray.
See if there be
Some wicked way in me.
Cleanse me from every sin
And set me free.

It was an unusual hymn, something she had never encountered before, and certainly not one of the old standbys that the congregation would feel comfortable singing. In fact, most of the voices simply chanted the words without following the melody. But she understood quickly that this eccentric choice could have been directed at her — or at least at all of them on Golf View Court. And Reverend Whitehead, instead of being apologetic for his role in spreading gossip (she was sure now), had turned aggressive. She would stay only long enough to hear the first part of his sermon and walk out if she had to. After all, she concluded, the members of the congregation weren't really shunning her; they were actually afraid of her, and she rather liked the thought.

After the hymn, which neither the choir nor the congregation sang with gusto, a long prayer and then a Bach piece sung by an ensemble of boys and men, Reverend Whitehead stood, gathered in his white robes with one hand and mounted the three steps up to the pulpit. His eyes swept over the audience and paused when he saw Marie sitting alone, surrounded by empty space. He revealed no emotion but began:

"What God knows? God knows what? What knoweth the Lord? The answer to this question is the simplest axiom of the Bible. He knows everything; every human soul is an open book to him. You cannot hide your thoughts by closing the cover of your heart, by convincing yourself that you are somehow pure and hidden from the reach of his searching eyes. No, he knows all; he sees all; and he judges all. And most importantly, he is the only source of forgiveness. No human has that greatest of powers: divine forgiveness.

"And just what is it that he sees? Not just deeds, for human actions can obfuscate and confuse. We all do things for a variety of reasons and a multitude of motivations. So the act is diminished in importance beside the intent, the pure desire to do good or to sin. That, my friends, is the difference between us and our Catholic brethren, who put so much emphasis upon charity and the easy confession to a priest. 'Judge not that ye may not be judged.' Well, yes, of course you might think that. But the secret meaning of that command lies in human motivation, for we can never be sure, just by looking at the actions of others, why they did something or what they might have intended. But God understands and judges our intentions, and even when we do not act, even if we only imagine breaking his covenants, even if we only whisper our desires in an empty room and never fulfill them, he knows and he punishes. He follows our glances; he senses the rapid heartbeat of desire; he recognizes and records those moments when we are tempted by betrayal.

"We live in a time of great danger and ominous threats to our happiness and well-being, to our very existence as a nation and, more immediately, to our community. For a healthy and happy community is the first, last and best bulwark against foreign evil. And those who intend to disrupt our community — note that I say 'intend' — are a greater danger even than the delinquent child.

"And what are these endangered covenants that challenge the nation and the community? I am not talking here about the ominous threat of foreign bullies and outlaws, of rockets and bombs, although these are serious enough, with their bluster and machinations. Instead, I mean the damaged sinews that bind our community together and its most precious institution: marriage."

Reverend Whitehead paused from his reading and looked at the empty space just to the right of Marie, as if she had an invisible companion, her true self or, she thought for a moment, her absent husband. He did not see the confused look on her face or the rapid transition of emotions that showed in her eyes as she considered whether to be upset or amused or simply appalled at his bravado. And then she realized that these words were uttered out of guilt for his role (or maybe his wife's role) in spreading the rumors that were disrupting the village. She also realized that there was nothing she could do or say to him now. He had much of the community behind him, and there was nothing to be gained from thinking that half of Potawatomi Acres was chuckling at the families from Golf View Court and the other half condemning them. At this point, it didn't matter.

She stood up, purposely knocking her purse against the pew in front of her to attract attention, edged out of the row and walked slowly down the aisle and toward the door. She could feel the eyes of the entire congregation staring at her. She could almost feel the waves of anger and shock beating on her back. Even Reverend Whitehead paused to look up from the sermon to watch, silently, the cause of the commotion of turned heads and whispers. Only when she had exited did he resume his jeremiad.

When Marie reached the Buick, she fumbled with the keys to open the door because her eyes were suddenly glazed with tears. When she finally slid in, she sat with both arms hugging the ivory steering wheel, bowed her head and sobbed, as if this hulking metal monster — with its flashy red fins, white leather seats and chrome gadgets — could protect and comfort her. Why, she asked herself, had she come in the first place? What had she hoped to discover when she knew what would happen?

~~~

Sunday hadn't erased any of the confused emotions Steve felt, and the empty house, with Celia gone, seemed gloomy and unreal. He could not remember what he had done to pass the time except for eating a couple of meals that he concocted out of leftovers and sandwiches, downed with several beers. He had been tempted to call Teddy Barr just out of curiosity but decided against it, preferring not to discuss his wife's departure. It would be, he thought, a sign of weakness. There had been a football game on the radio, but he'd had a hard time concentrating, even though it was his favorite team, the Chicago Bears, and he couldn't even remember the outcome, let alone the score. Nonetheless, on Sunday night, he went to bed exhausted, as if he had exerted himself all day, stretched between feeling alternately giddy and sorry for himself. When he awoke the next morning, he knew he had dreamed but could remember nothing. He just had the vague feeling that his mind had raced the entire night and that whatever adventures he had imagined would remain just below the surface like a body thrashing around under a bedsheet. He was not used to confronting his feelings. Perhaps that was why his dreams were only a stressful mystery.

Sitting in his office at the bank, on the far corner of the small park to the north of the train station in Potawatomi Acres, Steve looked out the window, staring at nothing in particular, until he relaxed his focus and the remaining autumn leaves became a red-and-yellow blur, as if he were regarding the prospect through a rain-streaked windshield. He shook his head, and the scene in front of him sharpened again, making him conscious of the faint sound of traffic as cars whooshed around the village center. With his own lethargy and lightheadedness, he could scarcely imagine the intensity and purposefulness of the morning traffic. There were shoppers looking for parking, delivery trucks, commuters dropped off by their wives, a yellow school bus that belched diesel fumes out the back as it shifted to slow down. Looking at the bus, he felt a wave of nausea or shame or guilt or envy — he could not determine which — thinking of his own failure and their failure as a couple to have children. And then he thought of his will, sealed in the large safe-deposit box in the vault next to his office. He had left everything to Celia, but now? What was the purpose if she abandoned him? "Or if I abandoned her?" he said aloud. Glancing down at his desk and the pile of mortgage applications and other loan requests, he sighed audibly. These were the contracts that bound up lives into unsuspected routines and permanency. Commitments to stay, to pay out over time, to live out an obligation — these were, oddly, he thought, a foreclosure on futures rather than the purchase of a home.

In such rare moments when he allowed himself to regret (when he was feeling sorry for himself), he thought back to his time in Italy during the war. He often wondered how his life would be different had he stayed on. Not that there was any romance to keep him there or really anything particularly attractive about a country that had invited such terrible destruction upon itself. But just to be different; it offered possibilities of the unknown, and he could have re-upped and stayed for another stint just out of curiosity. Why had he been in such a rush to come home, to settle down, to marry? Why had they all come back, jittery and feeling cheated and wanting nothing more than to catch up after their years of service? What was the hurry? He couldn't exactly remember. Perhaps it had been seeing so much devastation and death. Perhaps it was a delusion that America represented endless possibilities that drove him. But here he was!

And his next thought — his second thoughts — always led back to the decision to marry and move to Potawatomi Acres. He had done it for the golf, for Celia and because the city was dirty and raucous and becoming difficult. But now what did he have to show for it all? A botched marriage, relationships and friendships once so intense among the quartet on Golf View Court that they almost excluded anyone else — and those now shattered?

Sometimes he wondered about the lives of the young couples who came to his office to apply for a home loan. What sort of future were they purchasing? The same as his? There was a discouraging sameness about them that made him sometimes think that it was his paternal duty to warn them: "Don't live here! Don't settle into this comfortable compromise, this community of exclusions and prejudices." And then he would remember that even in this small community, there might be people whose lives were different — and perhaps valuable and interesting, if he would ever take the time to know them better than the worksheets in their financial profiles.

On Monday morning, Jim Reilly sat in one of the three booths by the plate-glass window of the Community Drug Store, sipping coffee and eating a piece of soggy, underdone toast. He had taken to eating breakfast in the drugstore lately to avoid Jordan's hostile stares. From his vantage, he could see across the street to the village commuter rail station, and if he squinted, he could see the sign over the tracks, which he knew read, "999 miles to New Orleans." Why that particular destination was highlighted was puzzling only to a newcomer to the town, for the through tracks of the Illinois Central led straight down the center of the state and all the way to Louisiana. "New Orleans," he thought. A place he had never been or even wanted to visit, with its swampy weather and spicy food. Not for him. Maybe Jordan would like it.

As he peered out the window, he could watch the assembly line of cars delivering husbands to the train for Chicago. When he saw the Clementses' big, colorful Buick pull over for Dan to hop out, he had a sudden sour feeling in his stomach and angrily pushed the chipped china plate, with its half-eaten toast, to the other side of the table. No one would take it away until he left, but somehow it made him think of the silent feud between him and his closest neighbor. He stood up abruptly, picked up the check that was tucked under his coffee cup and went to the counter to pay.

"Everything OK, Mr. Reilly?" asked the woman in the starched white uniform, her hair held up in a black hairnet under her white soda jerk cap.

"Everything as usual, Betty," he replied, looking down at the large badge on her breast pocket to remind himself of her name. He prided himself on knowing the names of the businesspeople and employees along the small strip of stores near his office. "Thanks," he added. "See you." He did not notice that she silently watched him as he walked to the front and pushed open the swinging door to step outside.

Up the block, he stopped in front of his office. It always gave him a jolt of pleasure to see his name etched in large gold letters in a half-moon across the large storefront window: "Reilly Real Estate." The alliteration seemed to him a natural and charmed title for his small business. Written below was a telephone number, and to the side, on a large easel, were black-and-white pictures of properties for sale, with the price, location and description typed underneath. He unlocked the front door and walked inside, going immediately to the back to switch on the overhead lamps. Because it was a sunny morning, they did nothing but erase the corner shadows, but he always believed that a bright room was conducive to confidence building, and confidence, he always reminded Jordan, was the legal tender of real estate.

He removed his suit jacket and hung it carefully on a hanger behind his desk and sat down. In front of him, there were several manila folders in piles, one of which contained information about possible forthcoming listings and the other 10 or so active sales prospects. He noticed that it was after 9 o'clock and Mrs. Stimson, his secretary, had not yet arrived. It was unlike her to be late, so he assumed she either was ill or had a pressing errand. She would, most likely, check in with him later. So he stood up again and walked to her desk to retrieve his calendar. There were two appointments scheduled for the day — one early and one around noon. Both were with potential clients. And the rest of the day, he could show houses if any prospects came by.

He went back to his desk and sat down again, leaning back on the oak swivel chair and pulling out a drawer so he could put his feet up slightly. He waited, hands behind his head.

By 10 o'clock, it appeared that Mrs. Stimson was not coming in for the day. He decided not to call her and turned to look through the descriptions of properties that he had listed for sale. They were widely dispersed in the village. It was a good sign, he believed — in terms of his name and prestige as Potawatomi Acres' leading (and only) Realtor — that he had business in every part of town. In fact, he reminded himself, in the past few years, he had sold most of the homes that were not handled by some larger Chicago firm.

Around noon, Mrs. Stimson suddenly appeared. She was full of apologies but offered no explanation for her late arrival. She quickly sat down at her desk and set to work. By 2 in the afternoon, Jim was convinced that neither of his appointments would show up, and he decided to leave the office for an hour or so. Mrs. Stimson could, he believed, manage any foot traffic that came by. And when he was bored or feeling insecure, he loved to cruise around town and stop in front of the properties he had for sale.

"I'll be back in an hour or so," he called as he left. "Nothing much happening today, and I want to inspect one of my properties again."

He headed first for Indian Hills, a small, slightly elevated area north of the Potawatomi Community Church. His property was on South Iroquois. As he turned into the street, he stopped in front of 215, the house for sale, but noticed that the Reilly Real Estate sign was missing. He noted that he would have to bring out a replacement the next morning.

From there, he drove about a half-mile to the next listing, on Elmwood Drive, No. 1001. Again he noticed that the metal "for sale" sign was missing. This time, he got out of his car and walked around the house to see whether it had blown down. He thought it might be lying facedown somewhere on the lawn. But it had quite clearly disappeared.

He got into his car and drove to the next property. This time, the sign was where he had placed it. But he had become suspicious and disturbed, so he went to each of his properties. After he had finished his tour, he counted four signs missing and six remaining. It was puzzling, but he decided he would come back early the next morning and replace them. When he returned to the office, he asked Mrs. Stimson to bring up several signs from the basement storage room so he could put them in the trunk of his car for an early run-by the next morning.

Home by 6, he said very little to Jordan and nothing at all about the missing signs. He retired early to his den and drank several scotches, thumbing nervously through the magazines that he had already read. The next morning, he woke up late with only a slight hangover. While he was dressing, the telephone rang, and Sammy began barking shrilly. He quickly picked up the bedroom extension, assuming that Jordan was busy in the kitchen.

"Very funny!" said Christine before he could even say hello.

"I'm sorry. Christine? Is that you? What's funny? What's the matter?"

"You," she replied vehemently. "Is it some kind of practical joke? Are you sending us some not-very-subtle message?"

"I'm really puzzled, Christine. Sorry, but I don't know what you're talking about."

"The 'for sale' sign you put in our front yard last night, of course! That's a lousy way to tell us to leave town. Who do you think you are?"

"I didn't put any sign in your yard. In fact, someone stole four signs from my properties yesterday. I was going to replace them today."

"Likely story!" she shouted. Then she hung up.

Jim was stunned. Only half-dressed, he ran down the stairs and opened the front door. There, in the middle of the yard, was another of the missing "for sale" signs, and he could see, across the road, another sign next to the Clementses' driveway. He didn't have to call Steve to know that he, too, had been visited by the phantom Realtor.

"Jordan," he called as Sammy began barking ferociously. "Jordan!"

~~~

The mail usually arrived around 11 o'clock along Golf View Court, but on this particular blustery November morning, the doorbell rang much earlier at the Barr residence, and when Christine, still in her slip and robe, looked out of the front window, she quickly realized that it was not their regular postman. His uniform was the same dirty gray with a black tape along the trousers seam, and the small truck, parked along the curb, was similar to what normally stopped daily. But it was a stranger when she opened the door.

"Is this the Theodore Barr residence?"

Christine almost laughed to hear her husband addressed as Theodore. It had been many years since anyone had ever called him anything other than his diminutive. It made him almost sound important to be called out so formally.

"Is Mr. Barr at home?"

"I'm afraid not," replied Christine. "He's already gone to the office for the day. Can I help?"

"You could sign for this letter, I suppose, if you are Mrs. Barr. And I don't suppose you'd be anyone else, would you?"

"No, I'm Mrs. Barr. I can sign if it's a special delivery letter."

"Nope," said the postman. "Not special delivery. It's a registered letter. But that requires a signature, too, just like special delivery."

Christine took the pen and clipboard that the mailman held out to her and scrawled her name across the receipt.

"Thank you," she said, accepting the letter, and she turned to close the door. The mailman backed off the front steps and headed toward his truck. Inside, Christine looked carefully at the package. It was a large manila envelope covered with official-looking stamps, with a letter, no doubt, inside. She put it down on the hall table for a moment and then changed her mind and then picked it up again. She carried it into the kitchen, where a cold cup of coffee sat on the table next to a plate that held smears of congealed egg yolk and the crusts of toast. She sat down and, without hesitating, picked up a knife and sliced it open. Reaching inside, she pulled out a single envelope with the emblem of the Fair Green Country Club in the top-left corner and a raised-letter address underneath. It was addressed to Theodore Barr. She paused for a moment, trying to decide whether the coffee was worth reheating, and then tore open the letter. She glanced down to the signature and saw that it came from the manager of the club. Then she read the body of the letter.

It was two short paragraphs but unmistakable in its intent.

"Mr. Theodore Barr:

This letter is to inform you of your formal suspension from membership in the Fair Green Country Club. Membership in our Association is and always has been contingent upon certain minimal community standards and upon maintaining a congenial atmosphere among the membership. Unfortunately, there have been a number of complaints about you from different members, which we take quite seriously.

You are, of course, quite within your rights to appeal this decision to the full Board of Directors, but I should advise you that I have already consulted with them and they are unanimous in backing my decision.

Sincerely yours,

Ed Thornton, Manager"

Christine put the letter down on the table and began to laugh — a slow, long, humorless snicker that shook her whole body. She absently picked up her coffee cup and spilled several sloshes of cold liquid onto the letter, staining it across the top half.

"I wonder who you offended, Teddy. Perhaps I can guess," she said out loud. "Well, you'll answer for it when you get home."

~~~

On a bright, windy winter morning a few months later, Candice Overmann opened her office door at the university after a long vacation with Mark in Sarasota, Florida. She sighed to see a rather large, untidy jumble of mail sitting in the middle of her desk, the accumulated deposit of a month's worth of correspondence, memos, student papers and academic journals. She sat down, wearily thinking of the need for answers to all of these requests and the time she must spend reading the dull essays that filled her scholarly subscriptions. Leaning forward, she began to separate the pile into three groups: those letters and memos she must attend to immediately, communications she did not recognize and the journals, which she would take home and thumb through during the long evenings when her semester's work would allow her the time. This casual triage occupied her for several minutes, and she scarcely paid attention to her task until she came across a letter with familiar handwriting. It was a bulky letter from Sarah. And then, suddenly she remembered that she had heard nothing from Golf View Court since her disastrous (she now admitted it to herself) interview/consultation with the wives; she and Mark had named them the "Golf View Harlots" in a moment of rather cruel and ironic hilarity. But she was very curious about what had happened and how the group and the community had eventually dealt with the scandal of wife swapping. She had assumed all along that rumors of the party would leak out and corrode the relationship this group had with the rest of the town, but she had no idea how it might end.

She tore open the letter and pulled out several sheets of stationery covered with careful, neat handwriting.

"Dear Candice," she read, "I've waited until now to write to you because so much has been happening that I wanted the dust to settle, so as to see things clearly. As much as it has, I think that now might be time, although I can't be entirely sure. Change, once it starts, seems to roll on with a momentum that gathers energy and speed every day.

"You wanted to know the results of your 'intervention,' as you called it once. I'm not sure of its success. In fact, to be frank, I fear you did considerable damage, although I know that this was never your intention. John and I rarely see the couples you met, and when we do speak, it is brief and uncommunicative. I believe my knowing what happened has turned them all silent — out of guilt or embarrassment. Anyway, I still drive up and down Golf View, and whenever I see anyone I know, I toot my horn, and they wave, but that's about all that passes between us. We really aren't friends anymore.

"You will be sorry to hear about Edgar Clements. You remember Marie. She's the one with the elegant clothes and the rather stuck-up attitude. Edgar's her eldest son. It seems he took their Buick convertible out late at night about three weeks ago, after everyone was asleep, and completely wrecked it. Rumor has it he was drunk at the time. Luckily, he was not seriously injured, although Dan Jr. (the other son, who was with him) was in the hospital for a few days with several fractures and I understand will have to stay out of school for several weeks.

"And there is more to report. In a rather odd, almost unanimous way, the community has turned against all four couples, and it's something that I don't fully understand. And against all of us, John and me included, I fear.

"For example, I've applied to increase the number of dance classes I will hold next semester, but the high-school principal has simply refused to communicate with me. I called him several times and wrote a letter with my request, but so far, there has been no response. I know that my classes are popular with the children. They are fascinated with movement and modern music, and if I do say so myself, I am very good at what I do. But I have the odd feeling that I am being ostracized, like these couples, for something that — as you know — never even happened.

"John is studying hard these days to learn about stereophonic sound, and he hopes to have some of the new machines for sale in his store next year sometime. I'm very excited to hear about it, too. It's a brave new world coming on, don't you agree? But I worry about his business, perhaps rather more than he does. He won't actually say anything, but I know that trade was down around Christmas.

"Finally, there are other dramatic changes coming to Golf View Court, not the least because there are two houses for sale on our street. I'll let you guess which ones. But I will give you a hint: One of them is the result of a divorce. And there is even talk of several Fair Green Country Club memberships being canceled.

"I have one further thought, Candice, something you should mull over before you put us all in a book or article, and that is simply to think about the times we live in. I don't have any bright ideas about how to interpret the world at large. I never did. But I will say that for all our (and your) concentration on psychology and understanding each individual and each gender scientifically, I think you (and I) have been dreadfully wrong. Something is missing from our analysis — something that complicates matters, something larger. And maybe you can think of it. But right now, I'm too exhausted to write further."

It was signed, "Yours truly, SARAH VOLLMER."

Candice took the three sheets of the letter and placed them carefully in order and was about to return them to the torn envelope. But she stopped, struck by a peculiarity that she had noticed almost unconsciously. She opened the last page again to look at the signature. Breaking off from cursive, Sarah had printed her name, her full name, in block letters as if there might be some mystery about the identity of the author. No, she thought, that couldn't be it; this change of key into formality was simply a dramatic way of taking an exit from their friendship. There could be no other reason for it. It was as good as goodbye.

She sighed, placed the letter aside in her "ideas" file and began to rummage through the rest of her mail. She would figure out another time how to write up her notes on what had happened in Potawatomi Acres — that is, if she and Mark ever decided to revise the new book on marriage.

~~~

About the Author

James Gilbert was born in Chicago but grew up duringx the 1950s in one of its outlying suburbs, very much like the one depicted in **THE KEY PARTY.** He received a doctorate in American history and became a distinguished university professor at the University of Maryland. He is the author of 11 books, several focusing on the history of the 1950s and one a New York Times "Notable Book of the Year." Despite his academic commitment to history, he never strayed very far from the belief that history and fiction are close cousins, each in its own way devoted to telling a complementary kind of truth. Being a six-time Fulbright visiting professor, a lecturer at the University of Paris and at Warwick University in the U.K., and a frequent traveler to Europe has made him particularly aware of his own American and Midwestern roots, as well as the singularity of American culture even in places that are awash with such franchises as Starbucks, McDonald's and American TV serials (dubbed).

THE KEY PARTY
is also available as an e-book
for Kindle, Amazon Fire, iPad, Nook and
Android e-readers. Visit
creatorspublishing.com to learn more.

o o o

CREATORS PUBLISHING

We publish books.
We find compelling storytellers and
help them craft their narrative,
distributing their novels and collections
worldwide.

o o o

17758600R00149

Printed in Poland
by Amazon Fulfillment
Poland Sp. z o.o., Wrocław